Mouthing the Words

Mouthing the Words

CAMILLA GIBB

CARROLL & GRAF PUBLISHERS, INC.
NEW YORK

First Carroll & Graf edition 2001

Carroll & Graf Publishers, Inc.
A Division of Avalon Publishing Group
19 West 21st Street
New York, NY 10010-6805

Library of Congress Cataloging-in-Publication Data is available.
ISBN: 0-7867-0852-2

_LO1998362_

Manufactured in the United States of America

To Ted

Acknowledgements

My heartfelt thanks to the following for helping Thelma see the light of day: Beth Follett, Ravi Mirchandani, Vanessa Kerr, Jonathan Sissons, Suzanne Brandreth, Dean Cooke, Ellen Flanders, Zab, Kenneth Grey and the Toronto Women's Bookstore. To my friends and family for their love and faith: Lorraine Segato, Sheila, Patrick and Edward Fennessy, Stanley Cole, Alex Gibb, Ted Colman, Lynne Fernie, Vibika and Lilly Bianchi, Anne Shepherd, Annie Sommers and Marnie Woodrow.
To Those who have offered their kind words and inspiration: Jeanette Winterson, Tomson Highway, Jane Rule, Jim Bartley, Martin Levin, Susan Cole, Martha Kanya-Forstner and Maya Mavjee.

BOOK 1

BOOK 2

BOOK 1

In an English Garden

This is where the man called our father comes from: he is sitting in a barn with his brothers Garreth and Timothy on a rainy April afternoon in the Cotswolds. Garreth, two years his senior, is home for the Easter Holidays, having just completed his second term at the Wheaton School. Mother Puff, named for the soft grey sponge of hair that frames her face, has been gurgling about her eldest—"isn't he quite the little gentleman now"—for the better part of the day. Five-year-old Timothy sits mute for most of his waking hours, his cheeks permanently inflated with a store of Liquorice Allsorts.

Douglas is in the middle—too young for boarding school, and usurped, in the candy-coated affections of his mother, by his younger brother. He is broody and introverted, with what will ultimately be his dramatic early hair loss already in evidence in the recession above his furrowed brow. Puff, by way of preventative measure, coats his forehead with an egg white every evening before Douglas says goodnight. In bed he dreams of being an allied bomber pilot and though out of dreamtime a real war is going on, there is nevertheless always an egg to be spared for Douglas's head.

This extravagance secretly infuriates father Hugo. Puff cracks a warm peacock egg over the rim of a white porcelain bowl and says, "Well, I'm going to see that our young Doug is the proudest peacock of all." As Gloucestershire's most esteemed ornamental bird farmer, Hugo trembles when he sees the fruits of his labour wasted on the thick skull of his middle son. He cannot argue, though, because this is, after all, a house dominated by Puff's repertoire of rather strange ideas.

On this particular afternoon—in one of her idiosyncratic and perversely well-intentioned attempts at parenting—Puff has locked the boys together in the barn. She has decided that the best way to ensure her three boys cultivate a lifelong dislike for the taste of evil is to let them spend several daylight hours indulging in gin and tobacco and making themselves "sick as sin."

While the details of what ensues behind the locked door of the barn go unrecorded in the annals of the collective family history, the irony of the endeavour is not lost on future generations. All three boys grow up to favour grain spirits over meaningful connections to other people.

Our father, Douglas Tate Barley, was the one of the three brothers conveniently blessed with initials describing what for his pre-teen children seemed like one of the more embarrassing side effects of his condition. Of course, we did for years think that all daddies shook.

Somehow all three of the boys ultimately marry, though not without controversy. Garreth appears to have married Cassandra because Cassandra used to be Douglas's girlfriend. At least it seems that way given comments like: "I did her a favour, Douglas. She was far too bloody good for you." Cassandra is from Australia, and this fact causes father Hugo to go to his grave saying things like: "We shipped her kind off to the blasted colonies for a reason."

Timothy asks Louise to marry him because (although he is admittedly enchanted) on the evening he introduces her to his parents, his father says, "Now that's a bloody gonk if I ever saw one." Surely the timing of this proposal cannot have been mere coincidence.

The man who is to become our father marries the woman Garreth is discovered clambering on top of in the back seat of his Rover six-and-a-half days after his wedding to Cassandra. Douglas has just been discharged from the army for some unknown indiscretion and he does not know what to do apart from getting married. Poor Cassandra attends the wedding of my future parents and appears to be the one most moved to tears by the sight of the lovely bride.

Rather cleverly though, my soon-to-be father has managed to marry the daughter of an RAF captain who he assumes will help get him reinstated. He is feeling rather proud of himself. Not only is there a potential job on the horizon, but he has successfully transformed Garreth's indiscretion into Cassandra's sister-in-law. Like his brothers, though, he is not free from the racist wrath of Hugo. With her long, jet black hair, his new bride Corinna is the object of slurs like, "We didn't win the bloody war so you could go and marry one of them!"

Lest you should think my future mother but a hapless pawn in this whole exchange, let me assure you, she had her own selfish motives. She positively relished the thought of her father and mother saying:

"Do you think this is why we sent you to finishing school in Switzerland?"

"This just can't be happening. The son of a peacock farmer, Corinna?" her mother sighed.

At which point my future mother tactfully responded, "Perhaps you could help him find a job, Daddy. He's just been fired from the army."

—

We trust that what we know to be normal is normal simply because it is known to us. Worlds meet in collision and the coherence of our histories crumbles. I feel it in the blank looks I tend to receive at dinner parties. When other people recount stories, I habitually interject with statements like, "Oh yeah, I know exactly what you mean. I used to feel just like that when my father held me over the bridge by my armpits." Eyes previously animated are suddenly staring soberly. "You know?" I might add hopefully. "That bridge over the Don River?" A gracious dinner party host might break the uncomfortable moment with some tactfully placed suggestion of more Stilton. And if I had a lover, this would be the perfect moment to give me a reassuring squeeze of the thigh under the table and whisper something in my ear like, "It's OK, dear. Just try not to talk." Often, silence has seemed like the only option.

I used to wonder if people actually did know what I was talking about and were just being particularly stubborn. At home later, I searched a mind of endless tangled fields of bracken and gooseberry bushes, whispering to my imaginary lover in the dark, to whom I described a silent, tiny, perfect world of strangers. "Haven't you ever seen it? What the world looks like without you in it? Hasn't anyone ever put you there?" I really don't have the words to describe it, perhaps nobody else does either, because no one seems to know what I mean. Maybe worlds don't exist without words.

Enough situations had arisen by the time I was a late teenager that I thought I just might call up one of the many excellent therapists who had been recommended to me. I had a stack of small pieces of paper with

names and numbers—notes handed to me surrepti-
tiously (and with alarming frequency) under tables, in
libraries, in banks and even, and especially for some
reason, at museums. I was going to ask one of these
professionals just what constituted normal. Being
wakened by your father in the middle of the night to
hold a sheet of plywood over a window as he nails out
the darkness?

So I met Lydia Hutchinson MSW who insisted on
hugging me at the end of every forty-five minute
session—a threatening gesture of outstretched arms
which I spent the next six days of every week dreading.
She encouraged me to work out my anger with the aid
of a plastic orange baseball bat the size of a nurse
shark, a photograph of my father poised on a bright
purple throw cushion ready for a good bashing. "But I
can't," I repeated each time. "Maybe I *am* repressed,
but in all likelihood, even if I wasn't, I hardly think this
would be the way I'd choose to express my anger." A
plastic orange object just wouldn't figure as a weapon
of choice in any of my fantasies.

"How would you choose to express your anger then?"
she prodded.

"But I'm not even angry!" I protested.

"But if you were?" (*Jesus, she wouldn't relent.*)

"I'd tell you to fuck off!" I exclaimed.

"Good!" she congratulated me. "A fantasy!"

"It's not a fantasy," I said. "I'm serious."

"Better!" she exclaimed excitedly. "Transference of your anger!"

I rolled my eyes.

She had a bit of a transference problem herself. She asked me if Christmas was a particularly tense time and whether my father had ever hit my mother while trimming the tree. I couldn't remember anything like that happening, and although it seemed possible, I was suspicious when she asked me if my father had ever thrust the silver star at my mother to deliberately pierce her hand. I said "no" and she said "the bastard" and we both looked a little confused. She seemed to have a fixation with fluffy white stuffed animals and because she didn't seem to be relenting on the idea that I take up the orange baseball bat, one day I suggested she take it and do some of her own bashing.

She offered to demonstrate. She picked up the bat and started rhythmically tap-tapping the concrete wall of her subterranean pillow room. She began lightly, but then worked her way up into a monumental crescendo in which she came out with the most startling range of expletives: "You mother-fucking-ass-licking-cock-suck-ing-shit-ass-bugger-squirrel-fuck!" Squirrel? I didn't like to ask.

I watched her in amazement and revulsion as she collapsed into her beanbag chair with her normally perfect French braid in tatters and a strange smug glow in her eyes.

"Was that good for you?" I mused sarcastically.

"So good," she sighed, and then burst out laughing. It gave me the creeps.

Needless to say, the experience left me thinking she was less than qualified to offer me much insight into the world of the normal. I had had enough trouble getting myself to her in the first place. Among my father's most persistent mantras were, "Cheese gives you nightmares"; "Red hair is a sign of inbreeding"; and "Priests fuck you up the asshole, but psychiatrists screw you between the ears." He had a pretty paranoid, acutely developed understanding of a master race of which he seemed to be the only surviving member. He was sure he was being persecuted by an alliance of Irish Americans and psychiatrists.

—

I was born into a crowded room at St. Mary Abbot's hospital, South Kensington, in 1968. Born in London into a month of nights and days only distinguishable from one another by degrees of grey. Born in a nation that regarded the delivery of new life as embarrassing and unseemly, that operated a National Health Service which viewed birth as a pathology necessitating a ten-day internment.

In Grade One, when I was given a fresh clean notebook in which to write something called "My Autobiography," I wrote according to the certainty of the collective narrative: "I was born purple and dead. I was born in England," as if to imply that birthplace determined birth state. In fact, as my mother describes it, it may well have. I did not burst forth into being. I was pumped into existence by a machine. Although I was the result of premature ejaculation, I was not overly excited about being released into the world.

There are no pictures of Corinna taken while she was pregnant. She was thin as a post and modelling for Debenhams when she discovered the speck within, and she viewed the assault upon her body as both career damaging and soul destroying. She was, however, able to take a certain amount of pride in concealing her pregnancy from the outside world. It was only when she was nine months pregnant and went down to the newsagent's to buy ten Mars bars at a pop that the truth was revealed. A well-meaning comment from the shopkeeper produced a scream of "Oh my God, I'm pregnant!", its echo still resounds throughout the streets of South Kensington.

Two weeks later I was reluctantly expelled—mangy and bawling in the bewildered arms of a woman utterly devastated by her demotion from model to mother. By the time Douglas came to visit, she weighed half a stone less than she had before she was pregnant.

"What can I bring you to eat, Corinna? What would you like to eat?" he asked her helplessly.

"What I'd like," she told him, "is a little bit of chicken," imagining something delicate and white, skinless, boneless, greaseless and divine.

He cooked her a chicken. Roasted it lathered in pork dripping and delivered it to her the next day in a brown paper bag. She took one look at the grease-stained bag and said meekly, "I'm sorry, Douglas, but I think you'll have to take it away." He wasn't sure if she meant the chicken or the child.

Corinna came home to a house Puff had looked after. "Looked after" was apparently a euphemism for making fudge and leaving sticky marks on windows, or burning pots when cooking eggs for Douglas's tea. Corinna was furious. As soon as she arrived she thrust baby Thelma into Puff's arms and grabbed the Hoover for a mad vacuuming as Douglas and his mother stood backed against the wall in fearful amazement.

After that Corinna took to her bed, hating husbands and babies and humankind in general. If it were later in history, someone would have suggested postpartum depression as Corinna thought aloud her murderous thoughts. She dreamed of burying her baby in the back yard. She dreamed of a sunflower rising in the very spot, dreamed of being deceived by its beauty, of feeling regret that perhaps her child might have grown to be as striking and majestic as this flower. But then it turned its face toward her and its seeds began to spill on the ground as it cried out in an eerie, high-pitched wail, "Mummeeeee!"

"Douglas!" Corinna screamed into the wicked night. "I can't stand it anymore! Get rid of it!" The words reached his room at the end of the corridor and precipitated her departure the next day. She would stay with her sister Esmerelda in Edinburgh and would he please *do something* with the baby.

What he did, as he always did, was call his mother. He drove baby Thelma to Puff and Hugo the peacock farmer's house in Gloucestershire. Puff was delighted by the opportunity to impose her underutilized parenting skills on her first grandchild. Hugo, however, was not nearly as pleased. "Rug rat," he muttered as he dragged sawdust from the barn across the carpet, coming in for his tea. "What are you feeding it our good cream for?" he'd shout at Puff. "That's like wasting roast beef on a bloody dog."

Eight months later, Corinna returned (a changed woman as the collective narrative has it), bursting to reinstate her claim on motherhood. She declared that her transformation was due to finding, on her return to the farm of her in-laws, that baby Thelma, pale, thin and toothy, had been tied to the bannister. "Bawling like a banshee, she was," Puff explained to Corinna, by way of justification.

But my mother, in her new-found maternal swell, defended, "It doesn't matter what she was doing. You can't just tie the bloody child to a bannister!"

"And a lot of nerve you have then, coming into my house and telling me how to look after the daughter you've gone and abandoned. Who's been up with the child in the middle of the night all these months? You're not fit to call yourself a mother!" my grandmother shouted.

"She's my child and I've come to take her home," my mother said, untangling me from the bannister and wrapping me in the wing of her coat.

—

Douglas had missed Corinna terribly. "Pussycat, we'll do what we can," he said. "We'll find a nanny if we have to. Hire some help." Much to his amazement, she replied, "I want another one. I'm afraid I've fucked this one up. Let's try again."

The truth was, her new-found maternal disposition had had its gestation elsewhere. In Edinburgh in fact, in the arms of a young solicitor with whom she'd had vigorous and indiscreet encounters for the better part of the last month. Her second birth would also appear to be premature. But this time she was ready, and baby Willy sprang forth according to script. Corinna leapt into motherhood with a vengeance. This baby would be different. It *was* different—the fruit of some undisclosed liaison, chosen, the affirmation of womanhood, the spawn of passion and secrets.

I was relegated thereafter to the realm of the rather inconvenient. But since my father lived in that realm too, I discovered an ally in him, and when I became two-legged and verbal, became useful to him as well. My job was to collect the chickens' eggs and help with the feeding of the pigeons. I called our garden the farm, although it was simply a garden in which we kept a small coop. We had moved from London to a small village called Little Slaughter, off the Hog's Back. We had moved there because my mother, being a rather spoiled daughter, asked Daddy for the down payment on a house. She was sick of the brown flat in London, sick of being reminded every day of lives she might otherwise be living as she wheeled Willy's pram past shop windows full of glamorous mannequins. "I could have been like that," she had sighed. Ah, to be thin, manicured and bloodless.

There were no shop windows in the village to remind her of anything but the grim present. In fact, there were no shops, no school or library, nor the faintest display of neighbourly goodwill toward the newly arrived family. There were seven small houses at the foot of a grand manor house and a tiny eleventh-century church. Ours was the smallest of the thatched cottages, shrouded in roses and wrapped in wisteria and so very very picture postcard English in my memory of it. But it was a house bought with Grandpa Harry's new money and herein lay the problem with our reception. New money was bad enough, but this new money was not even our own.

We were ostracized. There must have been some official village decree stating that the neighbours' children were not to play with me. My mother was terribly lonely without a soul in sight to be impressed by or adoring of her, so the task fell exclusively to Willy the cherub. My father drove the Mini to Guildford station every day and took the train into London where he had a job he described as "taking fat gits to lunch."

These he saturated with gin and tonics and then put on the train back to their wives in Hammersmith, leaving himself enough time for an hour's kip in the park before making his way back to the ad agency. He hated every moment of it, as he frequently reminded us.

We all sought salvation through imaginary friends. Daddy's was a secretary named Teresa. I knew, because sometimes he would come into my room at bedtime and say, "Let's play a game. Let's pretend we are at work, and I am your boss and you are my secretary named Teresa." He'd sit on my bed and I would pretend that I was typing. I liked to do that—my fingers tickety-tacketing across an imaginary keyboard.

"And what does Teresa do when the boss comes into the room?" he'd ask me. "That's right," he'd say. "She closes her eyes and opens her mouth and the boss gives her a nice kiss." And he'd stick his smoky tongue in my mouth and I would feel his bristly face. I didn't like that part, but I liked most of the rest of being Teresa. Especially when Daddy gave me a tiny bottle of perfume and said, "This is what Teresa wears. Why don't you put it on every night before Daddy comes to kiss you goodnight."

My mother had Peter. Peter was the pretend man who called her on the phone. I knew, because the phone would ring, "ring ring," and Mummy, still in her nightgown, would answer it and giggle low and wrap her arm around her waist and lean back in her chair and say, "Oh Peter." One day she saw me looking at her quizzically and said, after she had hung up, "Thelma—haven't you got anything better to do? You've got your imaginary friends, why don't you go and play with Ginniger and leave me to play with mine?"

"Is Peter pretend?" I asked her.

"Yes," she sighed. "Peter is pretend." And I knew what she meant. Pretend people were secret people.

I did have "better things to do," as a matter of fact. I had tea parties and burial ceremonies to attend. I had my imaginary friends—Ginniger, Janawee and Heroin, and Teddy and my favourite doll, Blondie, with the outrageous hair. It was my job to round up the silent troops, make sure their hair was brushed, and pour the tea. Little chairs were arranged around Bah the blue blanket, the table for the tiny tea service that soaked up its water and our conversations. Sometimes we played office.

A year later I was sitting in a waiting room by myself with some dolls I had never met before, waiting for Mummy to finish her doctor's appointment. I said to Ginniger, "These dolls are naughty secretaries. And you know what that means. Help me tie them to the chairs, Ginniger." We took off their knickers but there was no rope in the waiting room, so the best I could do was rip out some of their long hair with my teeth and tie them down with their own nylon fibres.

That night Daddy didn't come to say goodnight. He was busy with Mummy downstairs in the kitchen, dodging flying plates. "You bastard!" she screamed.

"Where the hell did she get the idea of naughty secretaries! What have you done to her?"

I hugged Teddy, and whispered to Heroin at the top of the stairs. "Oh no, Heroin, Mummy knows the secret. Do something." Heroin, as silent and stoic as ever, motioned to me to climb on her back. She is my horse sometimes when we are afraid and she takes me galloping so hard and fast that the ground looks like a green river. She has thick heavy hooves that crush flowers and bad people and when I turn my head to look behind us I see trampled irises and squashed brains.

Not only did Mummy know about the secretaries, but so did a psychiatrist named Dr. Reginald Knowles who watched me play through the glass at the Guildford hospital. Corinna took me there after her sister Esmerelda had been to visit. I liked Esmerelda. She was bigger and softer than Mummy, and her voice was sweet and soothing. She cooked Willy and me crêpes with lemon and icing sugar when Mummy was in bed having a migraine. And then she asked me, "What would you like to do today?" I led her by the hand into the garden and introduced her to the pigeons. There were twelve of them, special ones with Elizabethan ruffs around their necks, each of them known to me by name. She said nice things like, "Well, she's a pretty bird," and I said, "How do you know it's a girl?" and she answered, "Well, because it's so pretty."

"The girls are the ones with the tight fannies," I

pointed out to her, and then Auntie Esme said she felt a little flushed and could use a nice cup of tea.

In my bedroom she tried to squish herself into the chair that Janawee was already sitting in. "Oh no, Auntie Esme," I winced. "That's Janawee's chair!" I saw Janawee sliding down under the threat of obliteration.

Auntie Esme said, "Sorry, petal, can I sit in that one?"

"Well, normally that's where Heroin sits, but Heroin will sit here on Bah just for today."

"And who else have we got here with us?" Auntie Esme asked with interest.

"Ginniger. And Teddy and Blondie. Janawee's the baby so she doesn't talk yet. She doesn't even have any teeth yet. Heroin's the biggest. She is bigger than me. And Ginniger is in the middle."

Heroin was the biggest, the bravest, the most grown-up. She slept apart from us in the cupboard under the staircase and she knew the alphabet and copied down letters meticulously in a blue-lined book with MY NAME IS . . . written on the cover. Heroin was teaching me the alphabet, although sometimes she lost patience with me and told me that I was too old to "behave like such a baby," but usually she just nodded and shook her head without words.

Janawee really was the baby. She had shoulder-length blonde braids on either side of her head and a little pink flower of a mouth. She would only eat burnt toast with Marmite. She cried an awful lot because she was scared of almost everything and she was as small and fragile as a baby bird and slept nestled in my underarm at night because she was afraid of the ghoulies that lived under the bed. I was afraid of them too, and I would pull myself into a little ball so they couldn't reach out and nibble my toes.

Ginniger was, well, just like me. Somewhere in the middle. Sometimes a mother to Teddy and Blondie and Janawee, sometimes Heroin's baby girl, sometimes Daddy's naughty secretary, sometimes his pet, sometimes Mummy's little inconvenience, sometimes Daddy's little helper, sometimes Willy's sister, Auntie Esme's petal, or Grannie Puff's big girl now, but always rather moody and timid and quiet. She said very little and she rarely, if ever, laughed.

Although it was Heroin I talked to, it was Ginniger who just was. We never had to talk because we would only say exactly the same thing. There were either two mes—Thelma and Ginniger—or one me in two bodies, but either way we were inseparable and indistinguishable to others except by name. Only I seemed to know who was talking.

"We like to play office," I confided in Auntie Esme.

"And how do we play office?" she asked with interest.

"Well, Daddy is the boss and we are the secretaries," I told her. "And we do this," I said, pretending to type, to make the tickety-tackety noise of fingers moving across keys. "And we answer the phone and make cups of tea."

"Well, you must make a decent living," said Auntie Esme approvingly.

"Uh huh," I nodded. "And when we do a good job, the boss says, Well that's a job well done Miss so-and-so. Here's a little present for my helpful little secretary, and he gives us a new pen or some perfume and we thank him by giving him a big kiss."

"What kind of kiss?" asked Auntie Esme.

"Like this," I said. And I closed my eyes and opened my mouth like a goldfish, just like Daddy had taught me.

"Oh, that kind of kiss," Auntie Esme said knowingly. "But what happens if you don't do a good job?" she asked.

"Well, sometimes he says, Miss so-and-so, I think you've made an error in typing this correspondence. I think you'll have to lie down while I discipline you."

"And then what happens?" she whispered, her eyes widening encouragingly.

"I do what the boss says because that's my job."

"What's your job?" she prodded.

"Like I told you. Just typing and answering the phone and stuff like that."

"And lying down?" she persisted.

"Only when I've made an error. I do sometimes because like Daddy says, to err is human. And even secretaries are human. Even good ones are naughty sometimes."

"And what happens after you lie down?" she asked.

"Then I fall asleep and have a dream."

"And what's your dream about?" she asked gravely.

"About a flying insect," I said, sweeping my arm from the floor to the ceiling. "A dragonfly with a skinny skinny twig of a body. I am an insect floating up in the room and I stick up here," (indicating) "on the wall above my pillow and just look down. I feel very high up because I am only a tiny insect and I am afraid of being so high and my bed and the room look so big. And when the noise gets too loud I just suck in my breath really hard and my eyes turn inside my head and all I see is big red."

———

I felt very nervous after telling Auntie Esme. I knew I'd done a bad thing because the secretaries, like Peter, were supposed to be a secret. And now I knew what happened when secrets were broken. Mum threw plates at Dad in the kitchen and then she threw a chair and he said, "I think you've broken my bloody thumb!"

And she screamed, "How could you do this, Douglas! You're sick—do you know that—you're positively sick!"

"I'm sick?" he shouted. "What is sick is your prying little sister. What is sick is being dependent upon your arrogant bastard of a father—living here in this insipid little village pretending to be a couple of wealthy dilettantes when everybody knows I am just a slave earning a pittance in a dead-end job and you are just a spoiled bitch! No wonder she invents things—she hasn't got a bloody friend in the world to play with. Just her neurotic mother for company. What kind of life does she have? How can you make those kind of accusations? I can see where she gets her imagination—for Christ's sake, she even invents her friends!"

And then Mum was crying in her high-pitched wailing kind of way and Dad was quieting her, saying, "Pet. It's OK. It's OK. The best thing we can do for ourselves is get away from this place. Make a life for ourselves somewhere. Away from your family. Try to get a hold of yourself, darling."

I whispered to Janawee throughout this because she was crying and shaking in my armpit. "It's OK, little girl. It's OK. Thelma and Ginniger are here. We won't leave you. And Heroin will take care of us."

And then I was dreaming again. Dreaming a dream of a mouth that was trying to inhale the world. A bloody mouth in the dark ripping through the stitches that were trying to bind it closed. I was poised at its edge, holding hard onto Janawee with all my strength, trying to make sure we were not sucked in by the terrible undertow that sounded as loud as thunder. The sky was cracking with the noise. And I was holding on so hard that all my limbs got sucked into me so that I was a twig, a stick insect, catapulted up to the roof of the sky. Pinned to the underside of a heavy dark cloud.

Safe there, rigid and tight and looking down on the immense world below.

Animal Kingdom

"Your father has gone to Canada," my mother told me.

Was that like going to the office, or to Gloucester or London, I wondered. It was, apparently, only further.

"Remember the sea?" she asked me. "Well, the sea goes on for miles and miles and at the other side is another country like England, only it's called Canada," she explained.

I asked Heroin about Canada. Heroin consulted the World Almanac and told me Canada was the next biggest country after Russia, and that it had bears but it also had the Queen.

"Are we going to Canada?" I asked my mother.

"Eventually, Thelma," she sighed. "Your father's got to find a job before we can emigrate."

"Does Willy have to come?" I asked.

"Yes, of course he does, Thelma," she scoffed. "Don't be so stupid! We're a family."

"Can Janawee and Heroin come too?" I asked her with obvious concern.

"I was rather hoping we could leave them behind," she said. "You're getting a little too old for imaginary friends. In Canada we'll find you some real friends."

But I didn't want any real friends. I'd tried real friends recently. After Daddy went away, the two roly-poly girls, Bubble and Pink, started to come running up the drive to take me with them in the red Volvo to Creative Movement Class. Their mother, Mrs. Toddie, was round, with a big face like a treacle tart, and although I liked her, I didn't like being squashed between her pink fat daughters eating squashed-fly biscuits in the back of the vomit-smelling Volvo.

And I really didn't like Creative Movement. We were supposed to run around in circles in our slippers in the church basement, beating tambourines, or trailing burgundy ribbons while Mrs. Victor plinketty-plonketted on the brown upright. I preferred to sit under the piano, sucking my thumb and watching her feet push down on the pedals. I was afraid of these little girls, all their gleeful energy spinning them in circles round and round like Tasmanian devils.

On our way home in the car Mrs. Toddie would ask cheerfully, "So what was it today, girls? A little dancing around the mulberry bush?"

And Bubble and Pink would pipe in joyous unison, "Hula hooping!"

"And Thelma, did you enjoy hooping your hula? Or

should that be, hulaing your hoop?" Mrs. Toddie chuckled.

I said nothing and Porky Pink piped, "She's a wet blanket. She never does anything except suck her thumb and hide under the piano."

"Now that's not very nice, is it, Pinky-Pops," her mother gently chastised. "Thelma's just a little shyer than you girls. She'll come into her own. She'll probably surprise us all and grow up to be a famous ballerina," she said, turning round and smiling at me affectionately.

"Maybe she's retarded," mocked Pink.

"Yeah, maybe she's retarded," echoed Bubble.

"Girls!" shrieked Mrs. Toddie. "Now that is not at all nice. What do you say to Thelma?"

At this point I spoke for the first time, shocking everybody by staring Pink boldly in the face and saying, "Maybe you're a bloody bitch."

"I don't know where she gets this kind of language," Mrs. Toddie said to my mother with grave concern. "But I won't have my Bubble and Pink hearing those kind of words. She's obviously one very troubled little girl."

To this my mother graciously replied, "I don't really give a toss what you think. We're moving to Canada anyway, so you can just take your fat little cherubs and push off."

———

We got to Canada via some kind of drug-induced

sleep. We took a plane and half a Mogadon each, which for our little bodies induced a coma lasting about ten hours. We were carried groggily off the plane and into the arms of some man with a beard who we didn't recognize. When I started bawling in the face of this stranger I heard my mother say, "It's OK, Thelma. It's only your father." All I could think in my hazy atrophy was, Who's that? It had been over a year since we'd seen our father—a fifth of my little life, and this "our father" had a face that was completely unfamiliar. Perhaps it was the smile.

I woke up in a bed with a panda bear and my brother Willy. This was Canada. A bed and a panda bear and my parents somewhere nearby, going "blahdy blahdy blahdy blah" in a happy sounding way. "Yes, I am surprised, Douglas," I heard my mother say. "I thought it was all going to be skyscrapers and motorways. Yes, it's very pretty, and even a little garden . . . A fresh start . . ."

And scattered fragments from my father. ". . . the car. A perk of the job . . . A great country . . . anything possible . . . No one gives a toss here . . ."

There was a garden full of dandelions which it was my job to weed while Mum planted rose bushes and Dad worked on insulating our little wooden house. There was something called Kentucky Fried Chicken for supper on a blanket in the garden, where none of us were wearing shoes. I was listening to the voices of little girls echoing forth from the little wooden play-house in the garden next door.

"Because I said so. Because it's good for you. Because I'm bigger than you," one voice pleaded with another.

My mother watched me listening intently to the conversation next door and said, "Maybe they'll be able to be your real friends." I hadn't told her that I still had Ginniger, Janawee and Heroin with me, because that would have made her mad. The three of them had fit quite nicely into my little round white suitcase.

The girls Binbecka and Vellaine were having difficulty deciding who would be mother. Vellaine was winning because she was bigger and, as she reasoned, "The mother can't say things like, But I don't like it, it's yucky—can she, silly? So I'm the mother because you think it's yucky."

Mum went round to the neighbours the next day to say something like, "Can my little girl play with your little girls?" She knocked on the screen door and when she got no reply, called out, "Hello. Is anybody home?"

"Come on in," a woman's voice called out from the back of the house.

Mother tiptoed through, wrinkling her nose at the smell of patchouli, calling out, "I'm your new neigh-bour" as she made her way toward the sunroom in the back. "I'm your new neighbour," she repeated as she stared at the big bear of a man lying naked on his stomach on the linoleum floor – a tiny woman grinding her toes into his back.

"Releases the vitality of the chakra," she explained, working the knuckle of her big toe into the spaces between her husband's vertebrae. "You know—the life force," she said helpfully. "I'm Anika," she added. "And this is my husband Claudio." The man on the floor let out a groan of acknowledgement.

These were the first proper Canadians my mother had met and she was quite amazed. She introduced herself, explaining that she and her husband and their two children had just immigrated from England.

Another groan from the prostrate Claudio. "Can I get you some juice, or a cup of coffee or something?" Anika asked Corinna.

"No, really, I'm fine, thank you," she said, and was about to continue when in burst the two girls with their long tangled hair and their perfect white teeth.

"Binbecka and Vellaine," Anika pointed. "Girls, this is our new neighbour." She nodded at Corinna.

"Nice to meet you," Vellaine said out of breath. "We would shake your hand but we can't at the moment because we're horses and we only have hooves," she said, shrugging apologetically.

"Corinna has a daughter just about the same age as you two," Anika encouraged.

"Cool, mom," Binbecka said. "But we're just in the final stages of the show jumping competition," she said, cantering off to the kitchen sink to lap up some water with her tongue.

"Does your daughter have a riding helmet?" Vellaine turned around to ask Corinna. When Corinna shook her head, Binbecka said, "That's OK, she can borrow one of ours," before cantering out the back door.

"What lovely girls," my mother commented.

Claudio, who had by this time rolled over onto his back to reveal, without any self-consciousness, what my mother later referred to as a "plentiful fruit basket," said in a thick Italian accent, "Yes. Lovely girls. Lovely horses, lovely mermaids, lovely leprechauns and even occasionally lovely pirates."

Corinna tried her best to look neutral and maintain eye contact, but she was, I'm afraid, terribly terribly English. She and Douglas wore more clothes to bed than Claudio and Anika appeared to wear in the middle of the afternoon. She and Douglas slept in separate beds, because, as I later once heard my father explain to a colleague, "women smell." What a brave new world, my mother thought as she suggested bringing Thelma round to meet Binbecka and Vellaine.

—

I spied on the girls who were going to be my real friends through the slats in the fence. They were cantering over a series of chairs and skipping ropes that had been arranged in a circle around the back yard. At the end of each round they would scribble a number into the earth—ten points, less one for each jump they missed.

"And today, we have an appreciative international audience," Vellaine called backwards to Binbecka in mid-flight in her grown-up commentator's voice.

"We'd like to welcome our foreign visitor to the equestrian world's finest event," she went on, and then startled me by running straight up to the fence, pressing her face against the wooden board, and meeting my eye. "Perhaps you would care to come out of hiding and join us," she suggested in a whisper.

"But I don't have a hauce," I said meekly.

"Don't worry," she assured me. "If you can shrink down into the size of a kitten or a squirrel you can take the short cut and slip through that hole in the fence. Otherwise, you will just have to fly."

I was good at shrinking. In fact, I'd had years of practice turning into a stick insect, so crawling through the fence was something I found myself doing with relative ease. Once on the other side, I stared at the girls, their manes flowing in the breeze.

"First of all," said Vellaine. "In this country we call it a horse, not a hoss."

"A horse," I repeated diligently.

"Now, if you can turn yourself into a kitten, you should have no trouble turning yourself into a horse," she said decidedly.

But I couldn't begin to explain to her that I had actually turned myself into a stick insect in order to get through the fence. That was, after all, all that I knew how to be. I had no idea how to turn myself into anything bigger. A Shetland pony was about all I thought I might be able to muster.

"OK, a Shetland pony it is. But they're not very good jumpers. I just happen to have a little magic dust here, so I will sprinkle some on your heels and that should help you fly over the jumps," Vellaine said, picking up a handful of sand from the sandbox and shaking the special powder across my shoes.

"To the races!" Binbecka declared, sticking her arm in the air, and we were off. Vellaine followed by Binbecka followed by the Shetland pony. And the magic seemed to be working because I was flying over the jumps with grace and ease.

"I knew you'd be a natural, strange pony girl," said Vellaine as she etched nine points into a new column on the ground. "Looks like we have some stiff new competition, Binbi," she commented.

What a magical new world I found myself in—of special animals and plays and rain dances and television and soon-to-be school. Papa Claudio had built a wooden stage in the basement with a tree in the corner adorned with little red and white lights we could control with different switches. We performed plays there. Sometimes we performed ballets, and once we even made the room into a scary haunted house. Whatever it was, we charged admission and went to Mac's Milk afterwards with our earnings to buy Mars bars and Doritos and Coke.

We danced outside in our bathing suits in August

rainstorms, banging empty plastic Becker's milk jugs together and shouting "boinga boinga boinga!" We watched television and I became engrossed in the lives of new friends like Gilligan and the Skipper and Marsha, Jan and Cindy and the Captain and Mr. Spock.

My mother yelled at my father, who was disapproving. "I don't care if they are hippies, at least she's got some real bloody friends! She's hardly had a normal childhood with you as her father!"

But my dad really was disapproving and he started saying, "No more television and no more sleeping over there." Fine, I just wouldn't tell them about the latest voyage of the Starship Enterprise and I would invite Binbecka and Vellaine to stay at my house. But they didn't want to. In fact, although I knew they could turn themselves into kittens to crawl through the hole in the fence, they never wanted to come through to my side.

"You come over here," they said. "It's better over here."

The only time I ever saw them come near our house was on Sundays when my mum was roasting a beast in the oven. They used to stand by the extractor fan in the lane between our houses and say, "This smells a hell of a lot better than tofu."

"But I like tofu," I said. "And buckwheat honey and couscous and lentils. We never have those in my house."

"Precisely the point," said Vellaine, inhaling wisely.

"Well, why don't you come and eat with us?" I suggested.

"Because. We don't like it there. Your father is scary," Binbi said.

"Anika and Claudio wouldn't like it," Vellaine explained. "They've told us to stay away from him."

That confused me. I mean, I was afraid of him too, but no one was telling me to stay away from him.

"Maybe you could adopt me," I said one day to Anika and Claudio.

"Oh, I'm afraid we can't do that," said Anika, running her fingers through my black hair but offering me no satisfactory explanation. "But you can spend as much time here as you like," she nodded sympathetically.

"Like our other sister," added Binbecka.

I was afraid because Dad was angry a lot of the time. And blurry-eyed in the evenings, squinting at me over dinner and saying things like, "Isn't it past her bedtime" and "Don't feed her that—you might as well feed steak to a dog, that's how much she'll appreciate it."

Mum said, "You're sounding more and more like your bloody father every day. I thought we came to Canada to get away from him and now I feel like I'm sharing a house with him."

"No, as I happen to remember it, Corinna," my father objected, "it was your fascist of a father we wanted to get away from."

"Well, at least my father instilled something of a work ethic in me," she provoked.

"You!" he said, incredulous. "A work ethic! If that's so then you go out and get a bloody job! You see what it's like being an indentured labourer and having to support an ungrateful family!"

"And I assume that means you'll be taking on the job of parent?" my mother jibed. "In every job you've had since I've known you, you've become convinced that you are being undermined. You are a paranoid son of a bitch. As a parent, you'll probably think your own children are going to stage a revolution to dethrone you."

"All right, Corinna. As of tomorrow I will start washing their crappy nappies and you can go out and find yourself a nice little job. But don't come crying to me when you can't get hired because you're not qualified to do anything," he stated smugly.

"They're not even wearing nappies anymore, you stupid bugger, that's how observant you are."

"The only thing you're qualified to do is be a whore!" he shouted.

"You fucking bastard!" she screamed. The casserole went flying into the wall and crashed in the sink, and then a familiar silence, punctuated by Willy's sobbing as he clung to the leg of the kitchen table.

In the morning I had my nice school to go to. There I had my nice clean desk, and my exquisite penmanship to exercise in a nice new notebook under the guidance of my nice teacher named Mrs. Kelly. Mrs. Kelly gave me the book that was to be called "My Autobiography," in which I wrote, "I was a dead purple baby." She expressed some concern about that, but it was my next entry that prompted her to call my parents in for an interview.

"My name is Thelma and I am a dead, bled body or sometimes an insect or a rock in a cave. When I am a twig, my eyes turn around and I can see the inside of my head and it is red and bloody. My favourite hobbies are being a Shetland pony and coming to school."

Being anywhere but home really. Being in my imagination, or in another building altogether.

Dad was the parent now and Mum was getting on her fold-up bicycle every morning and riding to her job as a secretary at the Ministry of Transportation. Dad was sending me off to school with a piece of burnt toast and taking Willy to the Oriole Nursery School, where Mrs. Elkinburg gave him graham crackers and powdered orange juice.

Every day Willy brought home a picture he had drawn with crayons. Every day it was a picture of a blue dragon stretching out its red tongue to eat the sun. "He shows exceptional artistic promise," Mrs. Elkinburg wrote on Willy's first term report card. "His creative impulse, though, seems oddly fixated on the image of a blue dragon trying to consume the sun. He should be encouraged to explore other images."

"I think he's developmentally retarded," my father pronounced helpfully upon reading the report.

"Don't be stupid," my mother said. "The poor boy's starved for a little inspiration and encouragement. What does he see when he gets home from school? You. He might as well come home to a corpse. And Thelma's hardly any help. She's so lost in her imaginary world all the time, she thinks he's some kind of stuffed animal."

Mum only knew the half of it. I would pick up Willy from nursery school on my way home, and Dad would park him in front of the television and say, "Pipe down and don't bother me. Daddy has to help your sister with her homework. Why don't you try and do something useful like long division instead of your crappy dinosaur pictures."

"It's a dragon, not a dinosaur," Willy defended meekly.

And Dad said, "I've heard about enough out of you."

But Dad was no good at homework really. He always wanted to make it into a game, while I took it very seriously. He always wanted to be the teacher and whenever I tried to interject and say, "But Mrs. Kelly doesn't do it that way," Dad would say:

"But Mrs. Kelly's school is finished for the day. A woman can't teach you everything you need to know. There are some things only your Daddy can teach you."

Girl with a Suitcase

"It's a difficult transition," my mother explained. "Really, she's quite a happy child. You should see her at home." But Mrs. Kelly apparently wasn't convinced, because the next night Mrs. Allen knocked on our door and introduced herself to my parents as one of the regional social workers responsible for my school.

"Is there some kind of problem?" my mother asked, standing firmly in front of Mrs. Allen with a false and nervous grin, her "English face", I now call it.

"This is simply a routine visit," said Mrs. Allen cheerfully. "We understand that Thelma has been having a little difficulty with the transition to her new life in Canada, and we simply want to help ease the process in any way we can."

"Well, I think we can manage that quite well ourselves, thank you very much, Mrs. Allen. Good of you to show such concern, but Thelma's coming along quite nicely. Have you seen her report card? Excellent in every category, although she is a little introverted when it comes to interacting with her peers. Not surprising when she has been uprooted so dramatically, leaving all her old friends behind in the UK"

All my old friends? I lurked at the top of the stairs. Of course Mummy didn't know I had packed up Ginniger, Janawee and Heroin and carried them across the Atlantic in the little white suitcase that Puff had given me for the journey. So I piped up—"No Mummy, they're here. I didn't leave them behind. I was only fooling because I thought you'd get mad!"

"Sweetheart, shouldn't you be asleep by now?" my mother crooned strangely, turning her huge eyes round to glare at me. "Mummy'll come up and kiss you goodnight and help you say your prayers in a moment." Mummy will kiss me goodnight? But that was Daddy's job. And prayers? When had I ever said prayers in my life? Wasn't religion "a pathetic pacifier for weak people," as Daddy always said? I was very confused.

"Well, all right then, Mrs. Barley. Thank you for your time. But listen," she said, lowering her voice, "if you ever feel like speaking to someone, here's my card," she said, placing a small, white piece of paper into my mother's hand and closing her fingers over the top of my mother's with a small squeeze.

"These bloody North Americans!" my mother shouted as soon as she closed the door. "So concerned about other people's business and so . . ." she shuddered, "touchy-feely." She wheeled around, shouting, "Douglas, I hope you heard that. For Christ's sake, all you have to do is pack her a lunch every day and make sure she's wearing a clean shirt. Do you think I like spending every Sunday doing the ironing so that you all have clothes to wear? You could at least make sure she looks presentable when she goes to school. For fuck's sake, I can't do everything around here! Douglas, I can't cope! I'm living up to my part of the bargain and carting myself off to work every morning and still coming home every evening to wash the clothes and clean the fucking floors. I sure as hell don't want to find out that you aren't living up to your end of the bargain. I just couldn't cope with it. Where the fuck are you? Douglas? Douglas!"

—

I recognized the woman whispering to Mrs. Kelly at the door of the classroom the next day as that touchy feely Mrs. Allen who had come round to our house the night before. My mother had warned me, "If that Mrs. Kelly or Mrs. Allen should ever start asking you any questions, tell them they can go straight to hell and mind their own bloody business."

So when nice Mrs. Kelly put her hand on my shoulder and said,

"Thelma, my dear, this nice lady is Patricia Allen and she was wondering if she could have a little talk with you," I said:

"I'm supposed to tell you to go straight to hell and mind your own bloody business."

"Well, I trust the good Lord has other things in mind for me, Thelma," said Mrs. Allen, "and as a matter of fact, I think your happiness is my business." With that, she guided me off, a hand resting on my shoulder.

I looked back at Mrs. Kelly pleadingly and she pouted at me and mouthed, "It'll be all right."

What'll be all right? I wanted to mouth back at her, but by this time Mrs. Allen was suggesting we take a little walk around the playground together despite my protestations that I had a ton of math to do.

"You can get to that later," she said. "Mrs. Kelly understands." *Understands what?* I wanted to ask.

I sat at the top of the slide and Mrs. Allen sat at the bottom.

"Mrs. Kelly has shown me some of your autobiography," she began.

Traitor, how dare you.

"She's very impressed with your writing."

Smug swell of pride—*Oh really, is she?*

"We both agree that it shows remarkable sophistication for someone your age," she continued. "But some of the images are very disturbing," she said gravely. "Do they disturb you?" she asked me.

Mrs. Allen continued. "Where do you get such creative ideas, Thelma? Not out of thin air, I imagine."

"Just from my head," I said, not really sure what she was after.

"Most little girls write about their pets and their friends and their mummies and fairies," she said. "Not about blood and death and lungs and other parts of the body."

"But fairies aren't real!" I protested. I was getting frustrated and thinking this Mrs. Allen was perhaps just a little bit stupid. A couple of pork pies short of a picnic, my father would have said. I wanted to get back to Mrs. Kelly's class and bury myself in my arithmetic.

"Does Mrs. Kelly have a little girl?" I asked Mrs. Allen.

"No, she doesn't, dear, but I know she'd really like one. She really loves little girls."

So that was it. Mrs. Kelly was looking for a little girl of her own. And she'd chosen me! She was going to adopt me!

"Can I go back to class now?" I pleaded with Mrs. Allen, eager to be reunited with the woman who was going to be my new mummy.

"If you can promise me one thing, Thelma," she said seriously.

"OK. What is it?" Prepared to promise anything in return for this most joyous news.

"I want you to take this card. Ask Mrs. Kelly for some tape and tape it into the back of your autobiography. It has my phone number on it and I want you to phone me if you ever feel scared."

"Sure, OK," I said, indulging her. But why would I

ever feel scared or sad again with Mrs. Kelly as my new mother!

I went back to class all dreamy-eyed and full of love. In fact, I could hardly concentrate on my math, because Mrs. Kelly was sitting at her desk smiling sweetly from behind the cover of a book. I couldn't stop staring at her and when she came up to whisper to me, "Are we having a little trouble concentrating this morning, Thelma?" all I could do was inhale her lilac perfume and resist burying my face in her neck. I wanted to tell her it was all right, that she didn't have to pretend anymore, but I knew for the sake of the other children in the class that she must.

I loitered around after class, collecting brushes and erasing the grammar lesson from the board. I was waiting for Mrs. Kelly to say, "No need for us to stop by your house on Merton Street, your parents are quite happy with this arrangement, and I've bought you a whole new wardrobe full of clothes and shoes. Let's go home." But nothing like that was forthcoming. I offered to carry her books out to her Volkswagen Bug. She thanked me, and said she'd see me tomorrow.

I said, "Don't worry, Mrs. Kelly. I understand. Discretion is, after all, the better part of valour," and began trudging across the blocks toward Merton Street, leaving Mrs. Kelly to think: "What an awfully curious child."

Perhaps Mrs. Kelly is shy, I thought. Or maybe she has to ask her husband if it's OK, but just in case, I packed some clean underwear and a nightgown and Teddy and Blondie into my little white suitcase and shoved it under my bed. I had decided to leave Janawee and only take Heroin with me. Ginniger had virtually melted into harmonious existence with me, so there was no question of a decision to be made where she was concerned. But Janawee was blubbering so much that I said to Heroin, "I think one of us will have to stay with her—you or Ginniger—and Ginniger lives in my hands now and I'll need my hands in my new house." I was sorry, but Heroin understood because she was, after all, the strong one.

But every day of that week continued in much the same way. I loitered around after school and Mrs. Kelly smiled at me and told me she thought I'd better make my way home. To Merton Street, she meant. And then, because I was late and Daddy had been waiting to help me with my homework, he told me I was a bad pupil and I had to lie down and be disciplined. But I didn't care anymore. I let him do his disgusting things and I dreamed of Mrs. Kelly and thought, Soon you won't ever be able to do that to me again.

I pushed my Brussels sprouts into my mashed potatoes and Mum screamed, "Stop playing with your food, Thelma. You really do behave like an animal!" But I didn't care anymore because soon my real mummy would be coming to take me to my real home and she wouldn't yell at me like that. Corinna would still have Willy to yell at.

On Friday I thought, 'This must be the day because surely Mrs. Kelly wouldn't leave me at Merton Street for a whole other weekend. So I took the little white suitcase to school with me that day and Mrs. Kelly, who noticed immediately, held me back at recess to ask me what was in the suitcase. "A few essentials," I smiled at her conspiratorially and then ran outside to join the barbarians.

Outside her Volkswagen Bug that afternoon, I looked at her desperately and said, "But aren't you going to adopt me now?"

"Oh honey. Is that what this is about? You poor thing. Where did you get the idea that I was going to adopt you?"

"But Mrs. Allen said . . . " I bleated, tears welling up rapidly in my terrified eyes.

"What did Mrs. Allen say?" she asked me, grabbing my little hand in hers and looking at me with concern.

I could hardly speak at this point. I was trying to get the words out but my chest was heaving and my heart was pumping from my head to my knees. Tears were flowing out of me like a sprinkler. "But . . . I . . . I . . . I . . . thought," I struggled. "She . . . she . . . said," I stuttered, "tha . . . that . . . you," I sniffed, as Mrs. Kelly reached up to wipe the snot dripping from my nose. "Oh God," I wailed. "Oh God!"

Mrs. Kelly got out of the car and put her arms around me and I heaved against her there in the parking lot. "Thelma, I am so sorry. I can't adopt you. I had no idea. You have parents. You have a mother. And I have my own family," she offered, in an effort to comfort me. "Let me drive you home," she said as she put her arm around me and led me to the passenger side. She pulled the seat belt over my chest and wiped my face with another tissue.

But when we got to Merton Street I refused to get out of the car. "It'll be OK, Thelma," she said. "I'll come inside with you if you like."

"If I can't be with you then I'd rather be dead," I said, my chest still heaving with sobs.

"Thelma, I don't want you to be dead. I want you to be alive. It's good to be alive," she said. "It can be, I want you to remember that. Whatever happens."

I felt like screaming: *Please don't do this to me! These aren't people here. There are only insects in the air and things under the bed. There are only bits of people— bloody lungs swimming in pools of yellow and red and swollen bits hovering in space above me.*

My father opened the door to this: Me leaning back against Mrs. Kelly's thighs screaming, "NOOOO—YOU CAN'T MAKE ME!" and becoming even more hysterical at the sight of him. "YOU CAN'T MAKE ME!"

"She seems to be a little upset." Mrs. Kelly appeared to apologize to my father.

"What have you done to her?" he shouted.

"She just had it in her head for some reason that I was going to adopt her," she tried to explain. "When I told her I couldn't, she became very very upset."

"Pigeon," Douglas said to me. "Pigeon, it's OK, you're home now. Come on in with Daddy," he said, stretching out his arm, at which point I retreated even further into Mrs. Kelly's thighs and screamed a blood-curdling, neighbour-rousing, "NOOOOOO YOU BASTARD!"

"Look, I think you'd better leave," he said firmly to Mrs. Kelly. "Look at how much you have upset this child. I hardly even recognize her," he said with disgust.

"Perhaps I should come in," Mrs. Kelly said. "Just until she calms down a little bit," and my father had little choice but to agree as Mrs. Kelly held on to my shoulders and walked me into the hallway. I turned into her thighs and clung to them for my life.

"Come on and sit down on the chesterfield, Thelma. Try to calm down a little bit and I'll give you a treat," he coerced, reaching out to touch my back.

"I DONT WANT ANYMORE TREATS FROM YOU! I DON'T WANT TO BE THE BEST SECRETARY AND LICK YOUR STINKY LOLLY!" I screamed.

There was a moment of stunned silence before my father pleaded with Mrs. Kelly:

"She has an extremely fertile imagination. She has these imaginary friends, in fact sometimes she speaks to us in their voices and we think she might be schizophrenic," he rushed, pink and breaking out into a sweat. "She acts quite deranged sometimes—lying down on the sidewalk for no apparent reason and pretending to be a cat that has been run over by a truck. It has occurred to us that she might be mentally disturbed."

But now Mrs. Kelly was gripping me just as hard as I was gripping her.

Fork on the Left

I had, of course, "Gone and bloody ruined everything with my hyperbolic imagination," according to my mother. "She doesn't even know what's real!" Corinna shouted at Mrs. Allen. "And the language she picks up from those hippies next door—always exploring their bodies together as if it was a perfectly natural thing to do! No wonder she has trouble with reality."

It was my mother who had a problem with reality. She would have gladly served us marzipan fruit for dinner because it looked perfect, even if she knew it was ten years old and crawling with maggots inside. Faced with the alternative of having me taken away for psychological assessment and counselling, it was agreed that Daddy would go away for a while because "whether real or imaginary," said Mrs. Allen, "the child is obviously in considerable distress when in the presence of her father."

—

Now I had a key around my neck on a piece of string and although the responsibility rather terrified me, it gave me a new sense of power. "Who do you think is going to be the parent now?" was my mother's new refrain. I was to pick up Willy on my way home from school and mind him in the hours before Mum got home from work. Quite often this seemed to involve Binbecka and Vellaine paying Willy twenty-five cents to pull down his pants or smoking one of the Player's Lights my father had left behind. I ignored the others, took out the casserole from the fridge at five o'clock and set the oven to 350 degrees, laid the table, and pulled in the washing from the line.

Sometimes Daddy called. He'd say, "Are you being a good girl, Thelma, and helping your mother?"

"Yes, Daddy," I'd say. "Where are you?" I'd ask, and he'd tell me, "Winnipeg" or "Saskatoon," where he was "trying to get his business off the ground."

"But when are you coming home?" I'd ask him. "I miss going swimming with you."

"I don't think I've ever taken you swimming, Thelma," he said, slightly confused.

"Oh." Maybe he took Janawee. Or maybe Claudio took Binbecka.

I ♥

It is Christmas mid-1970 something. We are in a motel room in Buffalo, waiting. We have crouched low through the border, Willy and me sitting in the back of a van on milk crates, looking at the red balding back of the head of the man in the driver's seat. He has told us to imagine we are as tiny and quiet as insects. We are inhaling cardboard and pretending to be potato bugs rolled into balls, sucking in our feathery, numerous feet. We don't know this man. His name is Bernie and he is taking us to Buffalo. We are nervous and excited—having an adventure we are not sure we are meant to enjoy.

Mum has packed Marmite sandwiches, chocolate milk and Wrigley's gum into a Smurf lunch box and I keep telling Willy that we can't eat yet because we don't know when the next time will be. We chew gum and blow bubbles which we try to smack flat onto each other's faces, and then the balding, red-haired man glances over his shoulder because we are making too much noise.

We have had other hesitant adventures before this one. The last couple of years have included journeys on planes and trains, escorted by strangers and occasionally alone. This is how we get to Daddy. Waiting in lounges and motel rooms for white-shirted, coffee-breathing men to come and drive us further. Willy clutches the lunch box like a plastic talisman in his small hands.

The first trip was to Calgary, where we went to visit Dad on his business trip. Mum was with us then, saying, "Douglas, this really is lovely furniture," but I didn't understand why he needed all this new furniture when it was only a business trip.

This is Buffalo—hours and hours staring out a motel window watching trucks hurtle by. We don't know this place and Bald Red has left us with two cans of Coke and a wave over his shoulder. We are sharing one can, keeping the other for later.

Daddy comes with nightfall, sometime after we have stopped counting passing trucks. He pushes the door open abruptly. He is tense and wired and his energy fills the room and wakes Willy, whose head snaps from my lap. I am overwhelmed and nervous in the presence of this foreigner who takes ownership of us on random weekends and every other school holiday now. I move perfunctorily to try to kiss him hello but he pushes me away. Willy gets a handshake because men, my father tells him, do not hug each other.

This night is for driving. Blink blink of oncoming headlights, cigarette smoke and a drive-through truck stop where Dad orders four large styrofoam cups of milk. For later. He must have read somewhere that kids need a lot of milk. It is my job to make sure the milk doesn't spill, but I am nodding off, with my cheek stuck to the window and the door handle in my ribs, and he keeps waking me. "Steady the cups and keep me company," he says. "I don't want to feel like a chauffeur." He talks to me in order to keep himself from drowsing. He talk talk talks to me, big words and grand ideas and I am trying to make sense and be encouraging. He is inventing something—something that glues sheets of paper together and he's going to get a patent and make a million dollars. Last time it was a machine that stamped numbers on pages. Last time it was five million dollars.

We are eleven and nine now and beginning to know. We know that other kids don't spend their Christmas this way—smuggled across borders, hurtling through night on the highway gripping cups of milk between their thighs. The man we call Daddy who takes us away and we feel awe and love and terror: to do or say the wrong thing would take away the sense of security we are inventing here out of necessity.

—

Willy and I sleep on a mattress on the grey carpeted

floor of a house big and empty and smelling like drywall and new plastic. The woollen blanket is itchy and I hear the sound of snoring from the next room. Sometimes I hear weeping. This sparse house is one of several identical ones on an unfinished housing estate. Yet here we are in one of them, apparently living. There are only the two mattresses and a lamp on the floor. What's missing though, it seems, is not the furniture, but the feel of Christmas. I had not realized that Christmas has to be created, it doesn't just exist. I had never realized that somebody has to take care of the details and that by default it must have always been Mum, because Christmas wasn't here and neither was she.

Dad buys a tree. He buries its base in a mountain of nuts—brazil nuts, walnuts, hazelnuts, and almonds, and calls it Christmas on a desert island. He thinks it's very clever but I just feel terribly terribly sad and I am trying my hardest not to cry. There are so many nuts and we won't eat them all so it seems like a waste and they don't even look pretty there, all different colours of brown on the grey carpet.

Nothing feels right and I am walking through this empty house trying not to cry, watching my feet, trying to walk straight lines across the carpet but the lines become blurry with my tears welling up. Willy is crying because he wants to go home and Dad seems to be crying for the same reason. He is sitting on a cardboard box with his forehead cupped in his hand, staring at the ice cubes in the bottom of his glass, tears flooding down his cheeks, saying he misses my mother. We all want to go home.

On Christmas day he gives us each a canvas bag with I ♥ NY written on it. I have to ask what NY means and I am mortified by the big red heart because I know it means love. Inside is all this stuff, all this debris from my father's nomadic life. Paper and pens from trade shows and diminutive packages with tiny soaps and shampoos and toothbrushes from hotels and little plastic magic tricks wrapped in shrink wrap and short pieces of metal bound together in clever ways – brain teasers to be untangled. All this is thrown together and swimming in the bottom of bags with embarrassing red hearts.

We give Dad the cards we made at school, which I had tried to make envelopes for and Mum had folded into frayed blue towels. We call Mum at lunch time and I am trying hard to be brave, telling her "Yeah, we are having a good time. We went to a beach where there were crabs and Willy found a little seahorse." We had traipsed the north shore of Long Island that morning looking for treasures in the sand. We wore windbreakers and there were no people but we found surprises in the sand and wrapped them in sheets of toilet paper, which Dad carried in the pocket of his blue parka.

Later we ate turkey with salty bluish gravy and mashed potatoes in a truck stop full of old people hacking through the mucus in their thick lungs. Dad called me a hoyden and I didn't know what it meant, but I didn't like the sound of it. Then he asked Willy, "What are you planning on doing with your life?" Willy said maybe he'd learn how to ride a skateboard, but Dad got angry and said, "But how do you bloody well plan on supporting yourself, you idiot?" And then he was calling the waitress to fill his glass again, the ice cubes going clink clink against the backdrop of his sniffing.

We carried our canvas bags to school for the rest of the year, carried them so the hearts didn't face out, but carried them with curious pride nonetheless. I was proud because it meant I had a father. But the bound bits of metal that I could never untangle left me unsettled.

———

Mum started going out at night with her friend Pam from the office. We'd never known Mum to have a friend and never known anyone like Pam, and we'd certainly never known our mother to smear on thick silver-blue eyeshadow and wear silver slingbacks and go out dancing or to the theatre. Mum was getting "liberated" while Dad was getting drunk and sad, and it didn't seem altogether fair to me because Dad was all by himself on a business trip and Mum was here with us.

"I'm thirty-five years old, for Christ's sake!" she screamed at me between applications of liquid liner.

"I'm not dead yet. Why the hell can't I have a social life, too?"

Too? Who else had a social life?

"But what time will you be home?" I asked pleadingly when she and Pam were sashaying out the door.

"Relax, honey," Pam said. "Your mom's got a right to party just like anyone else," giving me an affectionate tweak on the cheek.

I liked Pam although my father would have said she was a flake. She was definitely cool, while my mother was still serving as an apprentice. Pam wore bell-bottomed jeans and Indian cotton shirts and smelled like cinnamon. Everything about her seemed to jingle when she moved. She had big brown breasts, which she liked to flash at me for shock value whenever I said something that struck her as particularly uptight or middle-aged. I said a lot of things then because I didn't like all the changes that were happening. I didn't like all this talk about sexual revolution and the battle of the sexes and nations and bedrooms because all I could hear was the sex in it. I had no choice but to appoint myself the guardian of morality. "What's with your Thelma?" Pam asked my mother. "She seems to have passed straight from infancy to rigor mortis!" she laughed.

"It's her paranoid imagination" my mother sighed. "Her grip on things has always been distorted, and Jesus, talk about melodramatic!"

So Pam took it upon herself to shake me up a little

bit and see if she could wring a smile out of me. One rainy afternoon on a Sunday in August, she and my mum and Rudy, who Pam referred to as her 'salacious lover', causing me no end of embarrassment, were sitting and laughing over tumblers of whiskey at our kitchen table. The back door and all the windows were open and the wind was blowing a sheet of rain across the blue and white linoleum floor. I was upstairs in my room trying to do my homework, but I was distracted by The Captain & Tennille echoing from the kitchen and by the fact that not one of them had made any attempt to bring in the laundry from the line before it started raining.

When I came into the kitchen, Pam was braiding Mum's hair, Willy was doing a puzzle, and Rudy was there with his feet up on the table rolling a big joint.

"What the hell do you people think you're doing?" I shouted at no one and everyone in particular.

"Having ourselves a party, girl," said Pam. "Why don't you come on in and join us?" she said, waving her arm majestically toward an empty chair.

"Because I am trying to concentrate on my homework!" I shouted. "And I can't work with this awful racket going on!" I said, crossing my arms. "And what's more, the Lord's day is a day of peace," I added.

"Jesus, Corinn—the girl's got religion." Pam turned to my mother in mock horror.

"What has gotten into you, Thelma? You were a

resolute agnostic until yesterday," my mother asked, bewildered.

Actually I had no idea who the Lord was, I was just looking for anyone to back me up. "What's more," I added, "drugs are bad and the next thing you know you'll be running around having orgies and talking about female organisms."

"Hilarious!" laughed Pam. "Lighten up, girl. Jeeee-sus. Where did you come from?"

"Well, actually . . ." I began to explain, before realizing that it was a rhetorical question because Pam rolled her eyes at my mother.

"Get a load of this," she said, moving to do one of her bare-breast numbers which was usually sure to make me leave a room in disgust and give my mother and Pam a good chuckle. She whipped up her purple t-shirt to reveal two smiling faces with big brown areolae for noses. I stared in amazement and she screeched, "Isn't it fucking hilarious!" and starting bouncing her breasts around so they looked like clowns bobbing up and down.

I covered my mouth with my hands, and my mother said, "Thelma? You look as if you're going to be sick," but when tears started running down my face it was Pam who said:

"Corinna, I can't believe it. She's actually laughing. Thank the fucking Lord, the girl's got a sense of humour after all."

My mother stared at me in amazement, saying,

"Thelma, I am quite sure this is the first time I've ever seen you laugh."

"Hallelujah for that," added Rudy, passing the joint to my mother.

—

Another man was sitting at the table with them the following Sunday. When I came downstairs to ask them to turn down the music and Pam said, "Ugh, Thelma. I thought we'd been through this last week," my mother turned to me all soulful and said:

"Honey, I'd like you to come and meet Suresh."

I could tell by her eyes that this was serious, so I just said, "On the Lord's day we take off our hats in the house," and stomped out of the room because I knew that would upset her.

I wasn't stupid. I knew from the turban on his head that Suresh was a Sikh, and that he couldn't very well take his turban off, particularly at a request to indulge some Christian Lord who doesn't even exist. But I didn't like the serious look on my mother's face. I didn't like the change in her voice.

Of course, years later when my father would scream, "That bloody Paki!" or "That fucking swami!" it would be me, not my mother, who would defend, "Suresh was a Sikh." But that was much later, and this was now, and I still had much too much of my father in me to believe anything other than, "We colonized the subcontinent."

My father, after all, had been discharged from the

army for calling a Visiting Official from Her Majesty's Royal Indian Regiment something similar. His racism was not reserved for a particular constellation of physical features. Red hair, he decreed, was a sign of inbreeding (which dismissed legions of Irish and Scots from respectability in his eye). Freckles and curly hair (I possessed a slight amount of both) were evidence of being "tainted with the tar brush", for which, in my case, he somehow blamed my blue-eyed, pencil-straight-haired, alabaster-skinned mother.

On the only occasion my brother ever brought a friend home to play, my father prevented him from entering the house by saying, "Where do you come from, boy?" To which the scared little soul replied:

"361 Balliol Street, Sir."

And my dad shouted, "No, you idiot, I mean your genes!"

Scared out of his wits, Willy's friend offered, "Maybe Eaton's?"

After his mother had called my mother to find out what possessed my father to be so mean to such a little boy, my father said dismissively, "I just didn't like the colour of his skin."

"Pardon?" my mother said. "Douglas, the boy is white!"

"But it's the kind of white I don't like. Pasty. It makes my skin crawl."

Needless to say, my brother never had any friends

after that, and neither did my father, come to think of it, or my mother, until Pam that is, and then Suresh.

Corinna's Armpit

The next Saturday morning Mum's bedroom door was closed. Her door had never been closed before and I knew this meant that Suresh was in there with her. My first reaction was idle speculation—was he morally bound to wear his turban while he slept? My next was sheer horror—there's a man in my mum's bedroom! There's never been a man in my mum's bedroom! Not even my dad slept in the same room. And what could they possibly be doing in there that necessitated closing the door? Disgusting! They must be fucking! He must be sticking his penis in Mummy's vagina! That's what fucking is! That's what Anika told Binbi and Vellaine and me and what they have been staring at Willy's willy for, thinking, How the hell does that work?

I was overtaken with panic. What to do? How to stop this ghastly moral infraction? I ran to wake Willy and yelled, "Mummy is fucking!" In his ten-year-old haze he looked at me as if to say, "And what the hell do you want me to do about it?" but really he had even less of a grasp on this fucking thing than I did. "Do something!" I screamed at him. "You're the man. Do something!" And when he just continued to stare at me, blinking his eyes awake, I stomped out of his room saying, "Ugh. You're useless."

I went next door. Anika was meditating on the afghan and Claudio was making griddle cakes for all of them when I burst in shouting, "Mummy is fucking!"

"Corinna?" said Claudio.

"Corinna?" repeated Anika, violently awoken mantra from a midstream.

"Gross," sneered Vellaine.

"Yeah, gross," repeated Binbecka.

"Can't you do something?" I pleaded, turning from Claudio, to Anika, back to Claudio.

"I can say congratulations," Claudio laughed. "Who would have thought."

"But it's morally wrong!" I objected. "She's a married woman!"

"Well, she's a separated woman actually," Anika corrected. "She's really at liberty to do what she pleases. And if this makes her happy, then that's good."

What was wrong with people? Nobody was on my side. I didn't like what was happening. Dad would be mad as hell when he came home and found another man in Mum's bedroom. Or worse, Suresh could have us all packed off to India by the time Dad got home. No, I didn't like the way this was progressing at all. And fucking makes you pregnant! I hoped to hell that Anika had told my mother, too!

"HEROIN!" I wailed at the top of my lungs upon running back into the house. Where was she when I needed her? I had left her for Mrs. Kelly and when I called her back and said, "It's OK, Heroin, I'm not leaving after all," she said, "Go gently into this good night, my dear. I shall never leave you, but hereafter I shall follow." She was always overly dramatic.

"Heroin?" Suresh pulled his lips from my mother's nipple to consider—

"Idolatry," my mother mused. "Her imaginary friend. I thought she'd given her up years ago. This doesn't augur well," she sighed, but added, "don't stop."

I paced in front of the closed bedroom door. "I hope you're using protection," I began. "I hope you realize that this is completely unsuitable behaviour for a woman in your position."

"And what position would that be," sniggered Suresh as he raised Corinna's ankle next to her ear.

"Suresh," my mother hushed him. "She might burst in here on her moral high horse. We'd better be discreet. She doesn't have any idea what she's talking about but the worst part is she thinks she does."

"Contraceptives are widely available over the counter at any pharmacy," I continued. "But just because they're available doesn't mean this is acceptable."

"Where does she get this language?" laughed Suresh.

"Her head. Her sophisticated neighbours. She reads everything. Digests words and then spews lines out as if she's written them herself . . . "

"I hope you've considered the potential outcome of this . . . "

"She's always got herself confused with other people. Whenever we used to address her as Thelma, she'd say, no that was Janawee, or Ginniger or . . . "

"HEROIN!" I screamed. "You came back!" Miraculously, in the midst of this crisis, Heroin appeared as my knight in shining armour to rescue us from this awful mess. "Do something, Heroin," I pleaded. "They won't listen to me," I whimpered.

But Heroin stood silent and resolute, perched atop her big white horse, which barely fit the width of our narrow hallway at the top of the stairs. I reached out to grab its reins, but despite its size in our tiny house the reins seemed to be just beyond my grasp. Frustrated at her lack of response, I bleated, "But Mummy . . . MUMMY . . . what about Daddy?" Tears were streaming down my face now. "What about Daddy? I miss Daddy. When is Daddy coming home?" I wailed.

"Now *that* is Thelma," my mother whispered to Suresh with a certain amount of relief. "Darling?" she called out through the closed door. "Thelma? Are you OK? It's OK. Mummy's here." But I wondered if it was really her because I had never heard such tender words from her before. I collapsed in a heap under the weight of those tender words, shaking there at the base of her door like a fallen lamb, blubbering my eyes out.

She opened the door then and used all her strength to scoop me up from the floor, carried me like a little ball because I was determined to inhale all my limbs, to be tiny and not let anything spill out of me, and pulled me into bed with her. When had she ever done this before? She had her arm around me and was saying, "There, there, pet," and I was trying to curl myself into her warm armpit because Janawee used to crawl into my armpit when she was upset.

I must have slipped into a coma of comfort for a few minutes because I remember nothing but the warmth and smell of her cotton nightgown, her deodorant's odour mingled with a peppery sweat. Nothing until she said quietly, "My friend Suresh was just telling me a story, Thelma, to ease my headache," and I looked up to see Suresh sitting there in his beige linen trousers and his white mandarin shirt with his turban and his beard, in the wicker chair by the window. Slouched down in the chair, gazing dreamily out the window, affecting what was probably a contrived but neverthe-less convincing aura of peace.

"Is it true," he said gently, his gaze not leaving the maple tree outside the window, "that there are no black squirrels in England?"

I peered up at his profile from the safety of the crevice I had nestled into between underarm and breast as he spoke the words, and thought, A nice face, a kind face, and I spoke a barely audible, "It's true." And he turned toward us then, slowly, with a smile, and the light shone against his teeth, a brilliant gold.

"Mummy," I whispered. "He has gold teeth."

"He does have one gold tooth. But you know his whole heart is gold."

"No," I scoffed. "How can that be?"

"You're the one with the imagination, Thelma. When did you start getting so practical?" she asked.

"I remember a little princess who almost lost her imagination once," offered Suresh. "In fact, when she lost her imagination she found she wasn't a princess at all."

"What was she?" I asked quietly, my curiosity aroused. Mum pulled my hair back behind my ear so I could see.

"She was just a mushroom in a field of other mushrooms on the estate of a very wealthy but evil king," he continued.

"Where?" I asked.

"Ceylon," he said.

"You mean Sri Lanka," I corrected him.

"Yes, Sri Lanka. But long before it was Sri Lanka it was ruled by an evil king who used to send his knights to dig up dead bodies and pull out their gold teeth so he could melt them down and fashion gold rings for his fat fingers. His hands were so weighted down by gold that he could barely lift them. His body was so fat that the island sunk a little further into the sea each time he took a step. And his face was so ugly . . . that . . . "

"Even the sun would hide behind a cloud so as not to have to see him," I added excitedly.

"Exactly," said Suresh. "You must have heard this story before," he teased, smiling at my mother.

"No, I haven't," I defended. "I'm just using my imagination."

"Which is what this story is about," Suresh continued. "Well, the evil king maintained his empire by sending out ships to capture slaves on nearby islands. The slaves were then forced to serve the empire, and if they disobeyed they were turned into mushrooms for the king's soup. After a few years the king, because he was such a disagreeable man, had many more mushrooms than he could eat in a hundred lifetimes of soup.

"Now most of these mushrooms had once contained human lives, but most of those lives had been forgotten. They didn't need to be forgotten, but living in the damp earth for so long, the people inside had forgotten themselves, forgotten their spirits, their essence, lost their imagination and the ability to transcend their present circumstances.

"Except for one little mushroom named Nemeni. Although it was increasingly difficult, she was sometimes able to remember a past when she had been the precious daughter of the good king and queen of the island of Sumatra—before the evil king sent his knights to Sumatra to seize all the little children there and bring them back to be his slaves in Ceylon. She was able to remember when she had been happy, when she had eaten rice with brown sugar. She was able to dream, there in the dank and stench of fields of identical mushrooms, of being human, of being real, of being free, and of being uniquely beautiful.

"Now the evil king had decided to spread a plague over his fields of mushrooms because he was overwhelmed (even though he was very greedy) by the amount of soup he had to eat to keep up with the number of enemies he was making. But Nemeni, who had the power within herself to imagine that she could be anything she wished to be, had a plan. She would turn herself into a poisonous mushroom and she would will the king to select her for his soup. She knew this meant that she would be eaten by the fat king and her own life would be lost, but in killing him she would save the hundreds of thousands of other lives contained in those fields of mushrooms."

"She was very brave," I marvelled aloud.

"And very smart, too," said Suresh. "For when the king drank his soup the night before he was to spread the plague, he thought with relief, This is the last mushroom soup I will ever have to eat, but little did he know it was to be the last time he would ever eat anything. He drank the soup like water because he was too greedy and lazy to chew. So Nemeni swam down his oesophagus, deep into his fetid stomach, where she spread her poison round like the rings of Saturn.

"When the king had swallowed the last mouthful of soup, he let out a deep groan of death, and a great burst of wind issued forth from his anus," [witness both mother and daughter giggling in titillation upon hearing this] "and Nemeni was expelled in one giant rush. Lo and behold, she had, in the course of her travels, transformed into a princess again. Before her, all the mushrooms began to rise up from the ground, bursting forth like new blades of grass, transforming into little people as they grew, each crying, "Nemeni. You are our saviour and our queen."

"But she was dismayed at the sight before her—hundreds of thousands of identical people, dressed in drab, grey uniforms, while she herself was shrouded in white and gold with perfumed jasmine in her hair. "I do not wish you to be my subjects," she cried out to the waiting masses. "I wish you as your dreams." And as she spoke these words the people began to transform into dreams of themselves: white knights and emperors and beautiful queens and friendly dragons and happy children, and mothers with babies, and lovers in each other's arms."

The air rang with the words of Suresh's story.

"The end?" I asked, uncertain.

"The end," Suresh nodded.

"But aren't you going to tell me, And the moral is . . . ?'"

"But you know the moral," Suresh said plainly.

"OK, then. But aren't you going to tell me something

like, 'And to this day, the people of Sri Lanka have never eaten mushrooms again.'"

"No, because they do. And they certainly know how to tell which ones are poisonous."

"Maybe you'll be a princess one day," said my mother, stroking my hair. "Of course you'd have to marry a prince, because you've missed your chance at being born into royalty," she laughed.

"But what if I want to be a lesbian when I grow up?" I said, breaking the reverie that had captivated us.

"Thelma!" my mother reacted, apparently shocked and embarrassed. She pushed me from her slightly in order to get a look at my face. "Where on earth do you get ideas like that?" she demanded.

"Imagination, Ma," I said. "The power of the mind."

—

Actually, Binbi, Vellaine and I had been hanging out at the top of the stairs one night when I heard Anika tell Claudio that she thought Pam was a lesbian. The next day when Binbecka asked, "Mom? What's a lesbian?" Anika said:

"A woman who loves another woman."

"Can I be a lesbian when I grow up?" asked Binbecka.

"Of course you can, sweetheart."

"Loves another woman like you love Aunt Irena?" asked a confused Vellaine.

"Well, no, not really. Not the same kind of love that

you have for a sister or a friend. More like the love you have for someone you are married to."

"Can I be married to you when I grow up?" asked Binbecka.

"Of course not, Binbi," mocked Vellaine. "Geez."

"Well, why not? I want to marry Mommy."

"That's sweet of you, honey. But I'm married to Claudio. And I'm your mother. And I'm sure you'll want to marry someone else when you grow up. And . . . (she was losing track of things now) I'm not a lesbian."

"I don't get it," said an exasperated Binbecka.

"Then what are you?" asked Vellaine.

"Well. That's a good question. I'm not sure how to answer that," she paused.

"Well, now I'm really confused," said Vellaine.

"That's OK, sweetheart," said Anika reassuringly. "Most of us really are."

———

So that was how Suresh came to live with us. Through a story, through imagination, through my mother's warm armpit. It still wasn't clear to me how Daddy was going to cope with this new arrangement. Suresh had gone so far as to throw out Mum's single bed and build them a new pine bed in the basement. A big double bed, in which there was room for all of us on Saturday mornings.

We would sit there, all reading different parts of the newspaper, and Suresh would explain things to me like the conflict in the Middle East and tubal ligation. He was studying to be a doctor and he seemed to me to know everything. He explained to me words like "carnage" and "genocide" and I told him that the rest of the world sounded like a horrible, horrible place and he told me that sometimes home could be the most horrible place of all and I knew that he was right. I knew that diseases started and spread outwards from home and that wars sounded like doors slamming and that the nightmares you could have in your very own bed were the worst places you could ever travel.

But we seemed to be happy now—Willy and me reading the comics and Mum and Suresh doing the cryptic crossword, all of us twisting around in the white sheets that smelled like bleach and bananas, for hours. And Suresh cooking in the kitchen in his white mandarin shirt and turban and sandals. Me rolling out the dough for chapattis, and the wonderful smell of lentil curry and cumin on spinach and potatoes, and even being given a taste of brown beer, and saying "How can you people drink that—it tastes like piss," and my mother saying:

"Thelma! For a girl with such a sophisticated vocabulary you do choose some vulgar words!"

"Sorry, Mum," I apologized. "I must have been mistaken. I meant urine," and she and Suresh laughed.

There was a lot of laughing in those days. And a lot of gardening—not Mum's precious roses anymore but sunflowers and tomatoes and green vines that spread over the ground and burst into long green and fat orange vegetables. And a herb garden, which was my responsibility. I liked slugging best of all—going out at night with the flashlight and startling the slimy grey slugs with the bright light and saying, "There you are, you sneaky bugger," as I scraped up another with my knife and deposited it in a bag of oil.

It felt like forever, like a whole lifetime, but in retrospect it was only a matter of a few months—a summer that flowed into an autumn which collapsed into a dark and depressing winter when Mum was crying a lot and Willy stopped talking and I looked round and round the house for Suresh but couldn't find him. I remember an evening when he came into my room and it was strange because he just crouched there in the corner watching me cut out pictures from a magazine for a collage I was making, saying nothing.

"Are you meditating?" I asked him, because he reminded me of Anika there crouched in silence, and he said cryptically:

"If only I could have such peace."

"Do you want to help me with my collage?" I asked him, hoping that would help.

"I am not an artist like you," he said sadly. "I am simply a puppet," he went on. "Not a free man."

I didn't understand and I looked up at his face curiously to see he was crying. I didn't know what to do so I just kept cutting out little pictures and gluing them onto bristol board and he kept crouching there, staring at the carpet.

He said, "I'd like you to have this," and he gave me a little gold ring that coiled round like a snake, just like the one he'd given to my mother.

"What for?" I asked, a little disconcerted.

"For a present," he said.

"Like a Christmas present?" I asked.

"Just a present for being you," he said, smiling sadly.

"Well, let me give you a present then," I smiled, getting up and rummaging through my toy drawer. Trevor the truck—no, I'd forgotten about him, he wouldn't do. Teddy? No, I didn't think I could ever part with Teddy. Blondie? Not much of a present for a grown-up man, I thought.

"The best present you could give me, Thelma, is a little gift from your imagination," he said.

I hadn't thought of that. What a wise man he was.

"OK, then. I will share Heroin with you. She is a brave Amazon warrior, silent and noble, and she will protect you from all evil," I said proudly.

"Well, that is truly the gift of yourself," he said.

—

It was years before I would really be able to understand. Suresh had finished his studies and was returning to work in India, where his marriage to a Sikh girl had been arranged many years before. "But why?" was all I could say, and my mother could give me no other reason than:

"Because there are some things about which we have no choice."

"But don't you remember Nemeni?" I asked her.

"I don't know. Vaguely," she shrugged.

"She could choose to do whatever she wanted, to be whatever she wanted to be, remember? Like a mushroom or a princess."

"Well, at some level maybe Suresh is doing what he wants," my mother said.

"I'm going to marry Suresh when I grow up," I said decisively.

"I thought you were going to be a lesbian," my mother sighed.

"Well, I changed my mind."

A *Stone Splits*

Mrs. Rodrigues had come to our school to teach us music—to conduct choir and orchestra and teach us mnemonics like Every Good Boy Deserves Fudge and Father Charles Goes Down And Ends Battle. I thought she was beautiful—tiny and perfect with nails hard as rocks that clacked on the piano keys, never chipping her beige nail polish. She was blond pouffy hair atop a sea of swirling beige. Hers was the white Trans Am in the school parking lot, and she spoke in a soft low voice. "I want Charlie perfume for Christmas," I told my mother when she asked. "Like Mrs. Rodrigues wears."

"You have a bit of a crush on her, don't you," my mother commented, and I was about to say, "I want to marry her when I grow up," but I knew my mother would say, "You're so fickle, last year you wanted to marry Suresh." She wouldn't understand that in my world I wanted to be married to all the grown-ups who had ever made me feel mushy, a category to which my parents had never belonged except for a brief flirtation with my mother during the time she had been with Suresh.

With Suresh she had suddenly blossomed into someone nice and beautiful. I see the photographs now and she is otherworldly, brown and curvy, standing in the dandelions in the backyard, swinging on the wooden swing with full, dreamy lips, flicking long black hair from her eyes. Without Suresh she was back to being her "bloody hell this and bloody hell that" old self, telling me that "life is hard" and "we're all alone in this world," moving distractedly throughout the house and getting thin. Without Suresh we were back to eating baked beans and fish fingers. Without Suresh we kept the windows closed and there was no more laughter. There was no more Pam, and no more Rudy, and even the stray cats seemed to disappear.

I imagined a life with Mrs. Rodrigues where I was her only daughter and I had a voice as golden as sunshine, a voice that moved her to tears. Mrs. Rodrigues was often moved to tears. She'd have the choir sing songs with lyrics that I found embarrassing because they were what my mother would have called, "touchy feely," brazenly Hallmark in their sentimentality, embarrassing because I could feel their romance in my stomach and I was sure it was obvious to others as the touchy feely rose in some kind of sexual/spiritual way through my body.

In anticipation of particular lines, I had the distinct feeling that I was going to become a frozen statue and split right down the middle. There were lines like, "If you touch me soft and gentle/ I'll show you who I really am and I will grow," which made me feel utterly mortified. Lines that I just couldn't get my mouth to sing. I resisted them by dismissing it all as yucky, pukey, touchy feely crap, and feeling utter contempt for the group of girlie-girls who would beg for Mrs. Rodrigues's attention at the end of class by bringing her flowers, writing poems for her, and asking for hugs.

I would never ever be as pathetic as that. No way. Instead I would daydream that my mother had been burned to death in a horrible fire, or crashed to death on Highway 401 and I would be left homeless (and Willy would also be lost somewhere in the great catastrophe) and parentless (it never occurred to me that in all likelihood if such a thing happened my father would probably take me), and that Mrs. Rodrigues would come to me (I would never go to her) and say:

"I have always wanted you to be my child. You have always been my favourite, special one, but I feared telling you because you are so brave and stoic that I thought you might reject me." And then I would say: "It's OK, I'll let you be my mother," (as if I was doing her some great service in making her life complete somehow) and go home with her to her nice condominium in North York and snuggle up on the couch with her and eat pizza and watch television.

I was not a snuggler in real life, I never had been. Except for nestling briefly in my mother's armpit one Saturday morning during the Suresh days, I had always been of the "don't touch me" variety, the variety that I realize now speaks loudly to sensitive teachers, social workers and psychiatrists of something being decidedly wrong.

I used to think it was because we were English and that English people didn't feel a need to resort to such perverse and primitive forms of communication as touch. I didn't respond very well to tactile gestures. I remember sleeping over next door one night and waking up in terror because Anika was rubbing Vick's Vapo-Rub on my chest while I slept. My heart nearly stopped beating. I swallowed all my limbs until I had turned myself into a brick.

I was getting good at this—I could transform into stone with minimum effort. At other times I heard a word, or breathed a smell, or saw the sun disappear in winter or nothing happened whatsoever and I turned hard, cold, without knowing, without feeling.

Dog Days and Ice

Daddy has come home. I am nearly fourteen. Daddy's home! Daddy's home? But we've been doing OK without him. Daddy's home? Oh God, I remember what it's like when Daddy's home. Corinna gets even more angry, Willy gets even more scared and I am no longer nearly fourteen anymore, I am a baby again, an insect sometimes, and in my newest incarnation, an icicle.

Why is Daddy home? Maybe Mum thinks it is better to be angry all the time than to cry all the time as she has since Suresh left, a long time ago now it seems. "Your brother's going astray," my mother explains. "He needs a father, a male role model. I cannot cope on my own. I just cannot cope," she repeats.

It was true there had been a couple of minor run-ins with the law, one involving a tape deck stolen from Radio Shack, and another a hockey shirt from Eddie

Bauer. The only difference between us was that Willy had been caught whereas I never had. I didn't think of myself as a criminal, or that my petty pilfering was leading me along the road to a life of crime: I simply thought I must stop this before my sixteenth birthday, at which point any juvenile delinquencies would be erased from my record. So because of some peculiar legality, Willy was a criminal and I was not. He needed a father, whereas I did not. As always happened in my family, something became a problem necessitating action only once the public became involved, so there were many more things housed between walls which never became problems in the same way.

—

I am fourteen and apparently becoming a "sullen and uncommunicative teenager", about which my mother said, "Hardly surprising. I could have predicted this. You look like you're back in your element. I'll talk to you when you decide to emerge from adolescence and be a human." But what she doesn't know is that have I resolved never to emerge, never to relinquish this new-found insulation, never to grow human.

—

At school we can get out of gym class by writing M beside our names on the class attendance list. It's easy. You just write a big M beside your name and you can sit out on the sidelines with all the other M signers. I hate having to take my clothes off and get into my bathing suit, so for the six weeks of swimming I write

M beside my name. The gym teacher, flaming red-haired, black leather-skirted Bunni Lambert, gripped her long, hard nails into my shoulder and said, "My dear. If you really have been menstruating for six weeks, I suggest you go and see a doctor."

Menstruating. I went home and asked my mother what it meant. My mother said with some perverse glee, "Oh, Thelma. It means you're a woman!" A woman? I think. How could that have happened? I've never wanted to be a woman. I am quite sure that I am still only a girl, a very little girl.

"Aren't you lucky you have me for a mother," Corinna chirped. "My mother told me it was a dirty little secret that one had to keep to oneself. I remember she told me the blood was a sign that my body had started to produce eggs. Of course, I didn't believe her. I mean, I thought it was such a ludicrous idea. I pictured myself laying an egg like a chicken in my sleep. So I got up the nerve to ask Jackie," my mother said quietly. (There were a whole lot of Jackie stories—Jackie had been Mum's best friend at school and she was much admired for being savvy and worldly-wise and wearing Chanel perfume from the Duty Free in Johannesburg.) "Jackie told me that my mother wasn't lying but the eggs are invisible. It felt like such a conspiracy.

"It was another year before I put it all together," my mother continued. "The book my mother had given me called *Where Babies Come From* and the eggs I would soon be hatching in my sleep."

"God, Mum," I responded to her story. "Stupid. It was just your period."

Perhaps I'd missed the point or spoiled her one attempt at female bonding, but she rummaged around in the bathroom closet and thrust a box of tampons at me.

"Thanks, Mum," I said. "But I won't be needing these." She does not realize that I have just decided never to have a period. No thank you very much, I am just not interested in going that route. You can take these straight back to wherever they came from.

"Well, what the hell did you ask me for, then?" shouted my mother.

"Dunno," I shrugged my shoulders.

"Thelma, you really are an odd bird," she said, shaking her head.

—

I have decided never to be a woman. Decided that I will be thin and little and rigid as a twig and hide in places out of sight from the world. I don't want to be sophisticated and wear push-up bras like Binbecka. I don't want to have claws and wear black leather and frighten children like Bunni Lambert. I don't want to have a stomach and cook dinner and lie back and say, "Oh, Douglas" with my father clambering on top of me and panting like a dog.

I daydream a lot about being an icicle: hanging from

the roof and watching the world, dripping away into watery nothingness in the spring. I want to come and go like winter, be unspeaking, cold and untouchable, crystal clear. No blood, no eggs, no stomach, no breasts, no claws, no sighing, no dogs panting on top of me.

"You should do something with your hair," Binbecka has started to say to me. "It's not becoming. Do something like mine. And clean your nails. What's wrong with you, Thelma? Don't you want boys to like you?" she asks me.

No. I don't want to paint my lips in Silver City Pink, pull up my kilt and fold it over at the waist, or press my face to the wire fence and giggle through to the other side. I don't understand this new language where I am supposed to say mean things about my friends like, "Oh my gawd, she's like, such a bitch," and then spend three hours that night on the phone with her talking about boys. I don't understand.

Binbecka tells me I'd better try to make some other friends because she has things she needs to do without me. There will be no more going to her house after school, making popcorn and watching The Partridge Family and me playing the piano while she pretends to be Diana Ross.

There is only my house now. Only my house and I don't want to be there. My mother is there pacing round the kitchen and rubbing her stomach. She looks at me like she's disgusted. "Thelma, what's wrong with you?" she says to me. "Don't you even want to try a little make-up? By your age I was onto my second bra. You look sick. For God's sake, you could at least wash your hair. Your father can't stand dirty hair."

My father can't stand. He can only sit at the table or lie down these days. After dinner, which I fold into my pocket and throw down the toilet, Mum sews in the basement and I hide behind my door writing poems. My father turns into a dog then and I daydream about being an icicle. Less dog and more icicle now. Every day less and more.

He follows me around the house and I can feel his breath on my back and he asks me questions. He tries to trap me. He asks me whether they are teaching me any English history at school and I answer reluctantly, "Only Canadian."

"That's ridiculous. That's not bloody history. It was the Brits who brought civilization to this place. I can teach you history."

Daddies teach you. Teach you about the white man and colonial conquest. Teach you lying down.

"Where's Daddy's little girl gone?" he coos at the side of my bed. "I miss my little girl," he says, rubbing his hand over his crotch. He is panting. "Don't you miss me? What's wrong? Do you have a boyfriend? Are you a little slut?"

*

I am otherworldly. I am where you cannot reach me. I am hanging from a roof forty feet above the world.

*

Panting is turning into spitting; coos yield to anger now. "You know, you look sick, Thelma. You look dirty. You look like a sick little dog," he spits. "You're lucky your Daddy gives you this kind of attention. No one else will. Even if you are a begging slut. Come on, Thelma, be good. Do this for me. Stop being so self-absorbed."

*

Drip, dripping, I am drops on a sunny winter's day.

*

"You know, I met your mother when she was your age. And she was a woman. She looked like a woman, she wore short skirts, and had those long legs and her thick black hair. You don't even have any breasts. You're a slut without the goods. A slut begging for this in your mouth. Come on, Thelma."

*

Clear, this sky is blue and I am shining, crystal, watching. Children reach up and out to me. Too high. I am dripping on their foreheads, they are stretching their tongues to catch me but they are missing.

*

"Come on, please your Daddy. No one else is going to love you."

*

I am rigid crystal glowing, giving rain, liquid silver. Water running over eager faces.

*

"You don't want me to stop loving you, do you, Thelma?" he pleads.

Pant pant, a Doberman loves a Pekinese. Jerk jerk thunder and flood. He's telling me I'm dirty and he thinks I might be contagious. "Your hair's starting to fall out," he sneers. "You're disgusting."

He knows nothing. I am growing, transforming, becoming hard as ice, and as shiny and beautiful and clear as pure water. Admired and untouchable. Brilliant and clean. Crystal perfect and loved. I am singing soundless. I am safe in isolation and distance. Nothing is here. Nothing is between me and the sky. Everything is below. Everything is dying below.

Burning

My father is gone again. Apparently. And I suspect this time it's for good because he was actually taken away in handcuffs. I have decided to feel nothing about any of this, nada, not a bloody thing, not even guilty, which is what my mother tries to make me feel because whose fault could this possibly be—except mine. Most things are, of course, and I have come to accept this quite graciously. By not speaking. No raising of voice, no anger, no defensiveness, just submission. It proves itself to be much simpler than engaging in fruitless debate. In arguing I always lose and feel worse. In choosing to remain silent I can sometimes manage to forget that anything at all has happened. Perhaps I am very English, after all.

—

My brother, who is becoming unknown to me because besides being otherwise disturbed I am preoccupied with being a teenager, has been sent off to live with our father. My father now lives in a farmhouse somewhere northeast of Brockville, and in their misguided way my parents seem to think a good dose of country air will be just what Willy needs to correct the unfortunate urban habits he is developing. I could have told them "like a hole in the head," had they asked for my opinion.

I know very little about Willy's life there because I try to block out as much as possible on my weekend visits. I cannot believe that I have to go at all, but "He's still your father" seems to be enough of a reason for my mother.

In this parallel universe there are a lot of fires. My father has some new-found pyro habit and builds blazing infernos that should have disastrous repercussions. But out here in the country no one seems to mind about things like fire hazards and clouds of toxic fumes because there are only cows next door, bony-assed and mooing.

Dad is apparently burning down all the old barns one by one, taking brittle grey planks and snapping them with his boot. The hay crackles and smoulders and crawls with beetles that go pop in the heat, which makes my brother say daft things like "neat."

There are gravel pits for miles here, most of them filled with stagnant green pools of water that teem with frogs at twilight and serve as an endless source of amusement for my brother, who seems to have grown an extra arm—this one loaded with pellets. It is May, and Dad is building infernos and Willy is shooting frogs in the middle of their foreheads, watching in morbid delight as they flip over backwards and land belly up. In January, when he arrived there, the water was frozen in the well and Willy had to crack it with an axe each morning so that Dad could have his coffee.

Now he goes to school on a yellow bus, which he boards every morning at the foot of the drive to the jeers of "Hey, stupid-ass," and "Look at his hippy hair, look at his stupid-ass jeans" and "Stupid Toronto ass with the freak father."

He does have dumb hair. Even I can see that. The wrong hair, the wrong jeans, the wrong words and a father who has started to tear down the walls of the house to stoke a fire. The other boys chase him in the schoolyard as far as the pine plantation and he shouts at them, "Yeah, well I used to be much badder than you when I was in Toronto, I even got arrested," and they mock him: "Stupid ass thinks he's a tough guy. Sure you got arrested. Arrested for being such a freak!"

He comes home from the school of abuse on the yellow bus in the afternoon to witness the progress of destruction. Dad spends the days alternately digging trenches with the back hoe and tearing off bits of the house. This is still my brother's most vivid image of our father—him perched atop a back hoe, with a gin bottle gripped between his thighs. Apparently happy.

"Look at this!" he shouts as Willy comes up the

drive, pointing to the day's destruction. Willy spends the next hour blasting frogs until it is time for him to scrub the potatoes. Always meat and potatoes. Wrapped in tin foil, thrown into the blazing fire and retrieved with a two-by-four. Sitting in the warm wind biting through the charcoal-skinned chicken to the soft red meat near the bone. It was only years later that Willy learned chicken didn't count as red meat. Years and a fitful bout of salmonella later. I avoid most things by professing to be a vegan.

Dad, of course, gets to moralizing in the drunken slurry speech that is his after dark. Moralizing about things it's taken Willy and me the rest of our lives to struggle to unlearn—about women, about life, about money, about women. Then it is bedtime. No dishes to do and no light by which to attempt to do homework. Just a stumble in the dark as Dad grips the top of Willy's head and relies on him to navigate toward the nearest gaping hole in the side of the house.

Willy and Dad survived winter with a wood-burning stove and a wounded house wrapped in tarpaulins. The cold months were dominated by a lot of moralizing and slurry speech which couldn't be interrupted by manic adventures with the back hoe. There was nothing for Willy to do except listen and pretend he was smoking, too, as he watched his warm breath meet the air. He cried a lot, particularly after the dog froze to death, and missed Mum, and said to me on my weekend visits,

"Can't you live here, too?" but I just scoffed selfishly and said:

"No way."

There were drives to the Texaco station for showers once every two weeks. There were snowstorms so heavy that Willy had to snowshoe a mile to the end of the gravel road to catch the bus, where they shouted "Hey, stinky ass" when he boarded.

And then spring came. Snow melted and the pits filled and it was April again and Willy had been living with my father for more than a year. Dad was a little better with the warmer weather because he could get back to work on his plans. He'd been talking all winter about the moat he was going to dig around the house to keep out government officials, health inspectors and Elmer Dixon, the farmer next door. There'd be a mechanized drawbridge for which he would have the only key and Willy would have a special code to lower the bridge when he got home from school. In the summer Willy would help him build an island in the government pine plantation. They would chainsaw down some trees and dig a big trench around the clearing. "That'll show the government," Dad said.

But sometime that spring the plans changed without anybody really knowing why. Willy got on the Greyhound bus going west and Dad went east, going nowhere. "I don't know, Mum," my brother said from a phone booth at the Toronto bus depot. "All he said was, 'Will, we're done here,' and then he drove me to

the bus station. 'Course that was after he burned the fucking house down." I picture it, everything at war. The flames and the rain and Dad and the world.

Years later Willy said a little more. He said, "You know, I should have shot that fucking bastard when I had the gun."

The Colour Purple

I am eighteen and I am still not adopted. How many people have I asked? It is starting to get embarrassing. Anika and Claudio, and Mrs. Kelly, and Mrs. Rodrigues, and then Mrs. Lennox my gym teacher, and Mrs. Abbey my math teacher, and then Mr. Foster my biology teacher, who took that as an invitation to stick his tongue in my mouth—and after that, well, that was only recently, but I've decided to give up.

Maybe I need to adopt something instead. I certainly cannot adopt a child, I have that much sense. But I could adopt a religion—except that a fundamental leap I just don't seem able to make has to be made in order to believe in a higher power. I have tried. I have tried meditating with Anika, I even spent the March break with Anika and Vellaine at a Sufi retreat in Florida, where I mumbled the chants and moved around in the circle with them, but alas, spiritual awakening is not to be mine.

My mother is having her breasts enlarged. I cannot believe she would do such a thing. Voluntarily add womanhood. It makes me feel sick, but she is glowing in some weird-ass way which suggests she is having her own spiritual experience. My religion will be based in my soul, not my mammary glands. I had always suspected she was superficial and vacuous, but somehow she needs to have plastic surgery and spend thousands and thousands of dollars to confirm this and worship her new God. His name is Warren and he is a corporate dentist, whatever that is.

He's harmless enough but he's made a few attempts at "Hey, I could be a father to you if you'd only let me in a little," which I have rejected so ferociously that he's retreated into remission recently. Like cancer. Which I guess makes me like radiation, an idea I don't altogether dislike.

As for my breasts, I am successfully suppressing all evidence of them and doing everything in my power to prevent a period from ever staining my life. I weigh one hundred and five pounds and I am five foot nine. My mother has taken me to the doctor, who has said, "She simply doesn't have the body fat to sustain the production of . . . " What? Blood? I know I've got plenty of that because sometimes I see how much I can squeeze out of the ends of my fingers. I haven't got the courage yet to take a slice into anything bigger, but I will, I'm sure of it.

I do weigh ten pounds more than last year, which although causing me no end of agonizing means my mother lays off, I can live at home rather than in a hospital, and I can think more clearly now. I'm not going that hospital route. Last summer I spent a delirious few weeks with an IV in my arm, staring at a bunch of other women with IVs in their arms, thinking: I am nothing like you, and being lifted onto a scale every day.

"Oh God, it's a morgue full of walking cadavers," my mother said, shuddering.

"Well, you put me here!" I screamed at her. "You wanted me to die in this graveyard."

At which point (and every other time I screamed at my mother), a nurse put her hand on my shoulder and said, "You know your screaming upsets the other patients, Thelma."

"Well, she upsets me!" I yelled. The nurse led my mother off and had a hushed tête-à-tête, but I was too exhausted to care about their conspiracy. I had to do most of my screaming in my head—holding my breath and clenching my hands and wondering if I could push so hard that my head would burst. I wanted it to burst—to shoot out my eyes and splatter its bloody red contents from wall to white wall.

Ironically, in my sessions every other day with Dr. Walker, where he actually invited me to scream, I thought, No way, you smug bastard, I am not going to indulge you, and I remained mute. I stared at him, I closed my eyes, I refused to answer his patronizing questions, and he said, "This isn't going to help you, Thelma. If I understand you better I can find a way of helping you so that you'll be well enough to leave here."

So he had the key and I was going to have to play by his rules in order to get myself a ticket. Fuck, I resented him for that, but I thought, Fine, I'll answer your pathetic questions, I'm a good student, I'll pass your test, and you can feel smug about having cured me but in actual fact I'll have told you nothing about myself. But I won't scream for you.

There was one woman I liked. Molly with the dead grey pools for eyes and long black stringy hair. I liked her because she always saw Dr. Walker right before me and she wheeled out of his office looking even more pissed off than I did. She nearly ran her wheels over my feet as she passed me, muttering things to herself like "dick head" and "Eat? Why don't you eat shit!" I stared after her with some degree of awe and fascination. One day she saw me looking at her, and mumbled, "I'm sure he'd let you out if you sucked his cock," and wheeled on by, not waiting for my reaction. Jesus, I thought.

Later that day she wheeled past my room and said, "Hey girlfriend. Wanna order a pizza?" I didn't know quite how to take that. Was she serious? But then she laughed and said, "Oh yeah, like that's exactly what I want right about now—double processed cheese and slimy, grease-speckled pepperoni."

"And only three hundred and ten calories a bite," I returned.

"Three hundred and fifteen, actually," she said.

"And maybe two Cokes to wash it all down."

"And a bucket to chuck it all up into."

"I'm not a big chucker," I said.

"Baby, it's the best."

—

"Did Dr. Walker really say that?" I asked Molly later, incredulous.

"Say what?"

"That you could get out if you sucked his cock?"

"What, are you crazy?" she asked, and then backtracked and said, "Oops, sorry. No, he'd lose his fucking job if he said something like that. I'd offer though if I thought it was going to get me out. Besides, he's got a nice little wifey at home who does that for him."

"Did he tell you that?"

"No. It's just that they all do."

"What a bunch of fucking pigs," I said.

"You said it, sister. Smoke?"

"What, here?"

"In the stairwell."

"Seriously?"

"Look, they've taken away one of my greatest

pleasures in life—barfing—they can cut me a little slack on this one."

"How do they stop you from throwing up?" I asked.

"They have a nasty little trick once you get on to solid food again. They inject dye into everything and it gets activated by your stomach acids, so when you chuck, it's purple. Your teeth and your gums and lips and everything. You should see the colour of my porcelain bowl."

"Cool," I said.

—

The next day she wheeled by my room and said in her best valley-girl, "Hey, like wanna go to the Eaton Centre today?"

"What, and go to like Le Chateau and buy a sequined mini so we can show off our, like, tooth-picks?" I asked her.

"And maybe a pointy-boobed Madonna thing to draw attention to our ample cleavage," she joked.

"Yeah, too bad they don't make them in a 28 double negative A." We laughed and I saw her teeth for the first time—yellow, grey and pointy, sticking out of her white gums.

"Then maybe we could like go to the Big Bop and pick up some like guys."

"And then what would we do with them?" I asked a little nervously.

"We'd rub our false titties against them and give them a big hard-on. The joke would be on them."

"Oh yeah," I said. "But what about our boyfriends?"

"Oh. You mean Surf and Turf? They've got a hockey game tonight but maybe they could come and pick us up at Sneaky Dees later in the Camaro."

"I hate that car," I said.

"Yeah, I know, it's totally embarrassing. And not much room for fucking in the back."

"Guess we can't fuck, then."

"Yup. Too bad, boys. It's OK," she said. "They're doing each other anyway."

"Yeah, I thought so," I said.

"Guess we'll have to do each other, then, if we want some," she said. That startled me. I didn't have a quick and witty response for that one. "Sorry," she said, embarrassed. "I didn't mean that. I was only joking."

The next time I saw Dr. Walker I told him that I was craving a Toby's Texicana burger. A big honking slab of beef on a white bun covered in thick smelly chilli. I told him Molly and I had a double date lined up for the day we got out of there—the two of us and our boyfriends seeing a movie at the Uptown and then eating burgers and fries at Toby's. No Diet Cokes with lemon or green salad with dressing on the side. Pure greasy suicide food. He told me I'd made real progress. I'd put on ten pounds and was having normal, healthy fantasies about food. I told Molly I'd found the key. "Tell him how much you're craving a hamburger," I encouraged her.

But somehow he didn't hear it from Molly in the

same way he heard it from me. He thought her version was a fantasy about friendship and living a "normal" life, she told me, and that the food was my fantasy, not hers. "How fucking dare he tell me that I don't really want a hamburger!" she yelled in frustration. "I want a hamburger! I want them to fry it in bacon fat! I want a side order of onion rings and a strawberry daiquiri! Fuck him!"

The truth was she wasn't gaining any weight. Every time her mouth turned purple they'd stick the IV back in her arm. What I didn't know was that Dr. Walker had told her she was using the food fantasy as a way to connect with me; playing into my fantasy in order to find a way to my heart. Hers Dr. Walker saw as a lesbian fantasy, while mine he seemed to view as an uncomplicated fantasy about beef.

I was allowed to go home but she had to stay. She gripped my hand with her claw-like fingers and said, "Don't you eat that fucking burger without me." I promised her I wouldn't. That I would wait as long as I had to. She stared straight ahead, gripped my hand and squeezed tears out of the corners of her eyes.

"You're crying," I said, surprised.

"I am fucking not," she said. "Don't look at me." She turned her face away and said, "I guess I am going to have to suck the old bastard's cock after all."

"That's not funny," I said, annoyed.

"Well, you did, didn't you?" she jibed.

"Molly, don't do that . . . "

"Well, why the fuck else would they let you out of here?"

"Ten pounds, Molly. That's the only difference," I said.

"You sound like everybody else," she said with contempt.

"Molly, I'm not like everybody else."

"Yes, you are. You give in, you play by their rules. You're so fucking straight."

"I have to go now," I said, seeing Corinna coming up the corridor.

"Yeah, fine, whatever," she muttered, her face still turned away from me.

"Molly, can't you at least look at me and say goodbye," I pleaded. "It doesn't have to be like this."

"Sure it does," she said. "No one ever fucking stays. People just lie to each other."

"I can visit you," I said hopefully.

"Yeah, I've heard that one before. Look, don't bother. I don't want to know you," she said dismissively.

"How can you do this?" I asked her, hurt. "I want to know you."

"Yeah, right," she scoffed. "This isn't a fucking movie. Forget it."

I sighed. "Bye Molly," I said, lingering for a moment. But still, she wouldn't turn around to face me.

My mother said, "She's an odd girl. She's a little queer, isn't she?" as soon as we got out to the parking lot.

"She's not queer!" I shouted at her. "She's fucked up, Mum. Who the hell wouldn't be after so long in there?"

"Well, I'm just glad you're not like that," she said.

"Like I'm so normal, Mum. Jesus."

———

I still lie awake every night kneading my fat in disgust and resolving to stop eating, but as long as I don't get my period I think I'll be all right. Molly doesn't write in response to my letters, so I guess she knew what she was talking about: people don't stay.

I will have to adopt something if no one is going to adopt me. I am too old for someone to ever want to adopt me now—although I could do a very good imitation of a gurgling and delightful baby if there ever was a realistic offer. Even Vellaine seems to have dumped the idea of having me as her little sister. She has waltzed into young adulthood in a way that is truly incomprehensible to me—of her own free will. She seems to be spending what strikes me as an unhealthy amount of time in paroxysms of delight with her new boyfriend, Charles.

I think Charles is a creep. Last year when my mother did the purge of "every stinking remnant in this house that has ever been touched by Douglas," out there on the pile, much to my horror (and Charles and Vellaine's delight), was a stack of seventies porno magazines. I was about to throw lighter fluid on the pile when Charles stuck his hand in and said, "Wait a minute, those could be collectors' items." Yeah right, jerk-off, I thought, and considered dousing him with lighter fluid as well. And then, of course, tossing in a match.

I don't care if Vellaine does love him. He is a creep and the sight of them flipping through those pages together and her saying things like, "Well, I can't say I'd ever thought of that," and him saying, "Wow," and them giggling together saying, "There's an option," made me want to torch her as well.

Fortunately my mother had the good sense to holler out the window, "I wouldn't be handling those things, kids, you don't really know where they've been. They probably come loaded with STDs." Vellaine and Charles both intend to be doctors, and they go around handling most things with latex gloves (including each other, I suspect). Corinna's holler brought them to their senses and they threw the magazines back on the pile.

"Geez, I never knew your Dad was such a perv, Thelma," Vellaine said with surprise.

"Yeah, well, who's the perv now," I scoffed.

"Don't react," Charles said to Vellaine, placing his bony hand on her wrist. "You know she hasn't been well."

"I wish you two would stop being so fucking smug and patronizing all the time!" I shouted.

Vellaine just smiled at me politely and turned to Charles, who had aspirations of being a psychiatrist, and said, "Oh, Charles. You're so good."

I had met enough psychiatrists by this time to know that Charles-the-creep would fit right in. Vellaine and Charles did eventually move to Moose Jaw to work with the native community as prescribed in Plan A. She and I were never really able to regain any connection to our earlier friendship until well after she had caught Charles "bonking" (being a doctor you think she could have come up with a more appropriate term) a native midwife, who, of course, he managed to get pregnant (um, excuse me, but how many safe sex educators does it take to get pregnant?) which led to his "relocation" and the subsequent disintegration of their marriage.

I would have been tempted to say "I could have told you so," but by the time Vellaine and I were reunited I had gotten over being so cheeky and defensive. In fact, she was busy asking me at the time whether I'd ever had sex with a man. I wasn't really sure why she was asking.

"Remember when we used to joke about being lesbians when we grew up?" she asked me.

"Yeah," I nodded shyly.

"Well, I think I'm grown up now," she said somewhat timidly.

So that was it. Vellaine was coming out as a lesbian. Thirty-three years old and a psychiatrist now with her own practice in Toronto and she was coming out as a lesbian.

"Why so timid?" I asked her. "You had free licence in

your house to be whatever you wanted to be. I remember Anika even explicitly giving you permission to be a lesbian if you wanted."

"Well, my house was not the world," she said mournfully.

"That's funny, I thought *my* house was the world," I said.

"I was ashamed of my parents. They were hippies. They were, you know, crunchy granola types. It was totally embarrassing."

"My God, I thought they were amazing. I mean in retrospect I have so idealized them—the openness, the affection," I said, amazed to hear Vellaine speak like this.

"Well, you know, too open, too unstructured sometimes," she said.

"Meaning?" I asked.

"Like they had an open marriage."

"Like sleeping with other people?"

"In theory. Although in practice only my mother did. My father remained absolutely devoted and monogamous until the day he died."

"Wow," was all I could say, leaving us both a little room to digest.

"But what about you?" she asked.

"What about me?"

"Are you?"

"A lesbian?"

"Yeah."

"No," I said hesitantly, although I felt like apologizing.

"I thought you were," she said, a little surprised.

"No," I said, shaking my head.

"But have you ever slept with a man?"

"Only my father," I said, shrugging.

"Oh God, Thelma." She put her arm around my neck and drew me to her until our foreheads rested together. Rested there together for a time in order to let the healing begin.

But that comes later. About twelve years and a whole lot of therapy later, in fact. For now, Vellaine and Charles are in the first blissful throes of their material union and I am feeling sick to my stomach.

Even Binbi seems to have defected. Although she was never the intellectual giant, I am really questioning her decision to be an exotic dancer. Well, not decision exactly, sort of default occupation while she auditions for positions as a proper dancer. Just as "no one's really a waiter," no one at the Zanzibar is "really" an exotic dancer. "No, really," insists Binbi, "the girls are all great. So-and-so is really a model, and so-and-so is really an actress, and so-and-so is saving money so she can go to veterinary school, and so-and-so has kids to support, and so-and-so is at university during the days studying to be a rectal optometrist." A rectal optometrist? One of them's got the wrong end of the stick anyway.

And what's so exotic about having all your clothes off

anyway, I want to know. People do it all the time—although normally in the privacy of their own homes. Quite frankly, I find it disgusting—morally reprehensible, but I have always been accused of being a big prude. Remember my mother's friend Pam saying, "Hey, check this out?" Even then I was a prude. But I'm English—what do you expect?

In fact, when my mother starts strutting her new surgically enhanced breasts around the house, nearly the first thing I shout at her is, "Mother! Remember! You're English!"

"This is the New World, honey!" she squeals, cupping her breasts in her hands with evident glee.

I am truly horrified. "But Mum, only last year you said plastic surgery was tacky, North American . . . " I say. "Common," I try, and am successful in hitting a nerve.

"Now that was below the belt, Thelma," she frowns.

"Well, if you don't find something to support them soon, they will be, too."

Oops! Mistake! Should not have said that, because then we're off on a mad brassiere hunt around Eaton's, Simpson's, The Bay (please God, when will this end?). I must escort her on this mission because I am under doctor's orders not to be left alone lest I try and hurt myself (although I think she could do much greater damage to me than I could ever hope to do).

My mother is saying mortifying things to saleswomen such as, "Before I was a C cup," and even worse, "Perhaps you could find a training bra for my daughter. I know she's tall, but she's really only thirteen."

"Actually, I'm twenty-five," I say, well within earshot of my mother. She is horrified and looks away quickly as if to suggest she was mistaken and we're really not related at all, but I continue. "Which means my mother is about *fifty* and I think she's having a mid-life crisis so just indulge her and tell her I'll be waiting for her in the shoe department."

She is furious with me, although she has, despite her intense anger, managed to purchase three new bras. Uh oh, and here she goes now with her "For once" speech.

"For once in her life your mother has a moment of happiness—why do you have to go and bloody ruin it!" I point out the flaw in her argument—if I added up all the "for onces" there would be somewhere in the order of ten thousand.

"You should be a fucking lawyer," she says contemptuously. "You're insensitive enough."

"I will be," I say, feigning nonchalance, although I have just, this very second, had a MAJOR BREAKTHROUGH.

"You what?" she asks, not sure if she has heard correctly.

"I'll be a lawyer. I'll be an animal rights lawyer so I can prosecute pharmaceutical companies that experiment on rabbits in order to manufacture that crap you cake on your face and produce those ridiculous silicone implants you're taking such pride in. Or I'll be a human rights lawyer and save children from parents who neglect and abuse them." Corinna's first reaction is to smack me across the face. Her second is to stand at arm's length from me and look at me like I'm a stranger. Clearly, she is relieved to hear that I have chosen a profession.

—

That was it for me. Since I couldn't be adopted myself; since I couldn't seem to embrace a religion or a lover because that would involve ghastly deeds for which I was quite unprepared; since I couldn't adopt a child, or a cause, or a nation, I became a lawyer, or rather, I adopted the idea of the profession. It would take me many many more years to actually become a lawyer. I still had all my madness to get through, after all, but at least the declaration was the start of something. While everybody was so preoccupied with their bodies—their breasts, their exotic dancing, their "bonking"—I would devote myself to logical arguments and Faustian bargains. Of course it didn't occur to me then that as an anorexic I was probably the one most preoccupied with the body. I thought I had tran-scended my body by refusing to yield to its basal demands. I wasn't really going to make much of a lawyer until I could come to terms with the fact that I inhabited both a mind and a body. At least if I focused my mind I'd inhabit something.

—

I worked extremely hard at law school. For the first year I was something of a fanatical student, undoubtedly annoying in the extreme to my fellow classmates, who probably dismissed me as a smarmy butt-kisser. I studied, I went to class, and I studied some more. I subsisted on black tea, Carr's water crackers and Marmite, and slept with the curtains drawn and the windows open in the depth of winter to prevent myself getting any more than minimal sleep. I ran up and down staircases in a paranoid frenzy and I studied some more. In fact, I just assumed everybody else was doing the same. What else was there, after all, to do?

Losing my mind was one possibility. And I seemed to do that with alarming proficiency as well, although I didn't know it was happening. I just thought I was too worried to sleep, too worried that I would fail, too worried about school work to leave the house, to answer the phone, or to eat. Everything in the outside world threatened to overtake me, to distract me from my new-found purpose in life. What was that purpose? I don't really know. But I knew the outside world threatened to overtake it. To overtake me, to envelop me in its huge, twisting undertow.

I got to my classes by taxi. In a taxi I could sit alone in the back and strap my seat belt on and lock the doors. I shook all the way, looked around nervously once I got there, balked at the challenge of small talk. I could hear my classmates talking. See them talking without their lips moving. Their voices were alive in my head.

"Maybe she's retarded."

"I don't know. Maybe her sister wrote her LSATS for her."

"I don't know. Something's definitely wrong with her."

"She probably just needs a good fuck."

"Well, I'm not volunteering to do the dirty deed!"

"I can't believe they ever let her in here."

"Does she stutter?"

"I wouldn't know, I've never heard her talk."

"Yeah, she makes weird noises."

"Like a dog."

"Or a cat in heat."

"And she smells like piss."

"Dirty."

"Gross."

"Who'd ever want to sleep with her?"

"No thank you."

"I'd rather fuck my brother."

"Don't you anyway?"

"Ha ha."

"We should get her drunk."

"Rip off all her clothes."

"See how many of us can fuck her."

"Make her scream."

My God, they were coming. Coming to get me. I

could hear them coming, rushing like a wave, whispering along the hallway to my residence room, getting louder and louder, and I was sure that I had forgotten to lock the door but I was too afraid to get out of my bed to check. I pulled the sheet over my head, and I could feel them breathing down on top of me—all the men in my class crowding through the doorway and the women not far behind, shouting:

"There she is."

"The little shrew."

"You have no idea what's coming."

"Not even in your wildest dreams."

And they ripped down the sheet over my face and exposed my skeletal body, trembling in its nightgown, and said, "Look at the delicate little leaf shaking in the wind / come meet your maker / look at the tree from which you came / look at this big tree / now suck it little girl / put this tree in your mouth and suck it," and my mouth is full of the hard and smelly and I am choking, vomiting, and it is pushing, thrusting through my vomit and then another one, spreading my legs and pinning them down and shoving inside, the pain, the burning, the rip, the rupture. "God, she's got a tight little cunt, no one's ever been in here before," and my whole body twisted, searing, flaming, flooded, flying, shrinking, inhaling, disappearing, up and up, away, floating, levitating, small, shrivelled, stick-like, watching. If only my eyes, if only I was blind, but the images are there, even when my eyes have turned inward, the people are still there. The people are rolling over my brain like they are writhing on a bed in hell, swimming in the blood in my head.

It is worse here, in my head. You don't need eyes and ears to be here.

Thelma of Distinction

It is a week after our exams. I am sure that I have failed. I am convinced I am stupid, have only the vaguest grasp, but I nevertheless drag myself to the law faculty on the day when our names, with pass or fail grades, will be posted.

There is a sea swirling around the board outside the Dean's office. A sea of rapists and cheerleaders. But I am here because I have a purpose. I am here to read my name under failure and then I can kill myself in peace.

I feel the sea part. There is a strange hush as it parts to let me through. Faces of rapists and cheerleaders stare at me and whisper as I move toward the board. I see my name there. Alone, set apart. I have failed. The only one to fail. But above my name it says, "With Distinction." Mine is the first name, and I am bewildered. I am perplexed. I run my fingertip over my name, mesmerized. Thelma Ann Barley. That's me, I think. I am Thelma.

I feel an arm around my shoulder. "You deserve it, Thelma," says a man's voice. "Yeah, none of us could ever keep up with you," says another. "Your dedication is truly inspiring." I hear the Dean's voice. But I am confused. That's me. I am Thelma. I am Thelma of Distinction. I am crying now, confused, and the tears are streaming down my face, but God, they are stinging so much I am wincing and can no longer open my eyes. I hear a female voice, "Yeah, it must be pretty overwhelming," but all I can do is scream:

"My eyes!"

—

It is a hospital. Evidently. You don't need to be a lawyer to figure that much out. It is me, waking up in a bed, but I cannot move my hands, because they are strapped down with white canvas to the metal frame of the bed. It is a doctor; no, two; and a nurse, and the Dean of Law, and God forbid, my mother, and some other people who look official.

"And what's your name?" asks a voice.

"That's a question from the movies," I mumble, and I hear my mother say with some embarrassment:

"Oh God. That's Thelma all right."

"Mum," I moan, "just get over it. Things seem to be past the point where we need to be embarrassed."

"She's quite lucid," says another voice.

"It would appear so," I say. "In which case, what the hell am I doing here? I feel fine."

"You don't look fine, sweetheart," says my mother.

"Well, my eyes hurt a little."

"We've put some drops in them and applied antiseptic cream over the scratches on your cheeks. Your hands are tied down to prevent you from touching your eyes or doing any further damage to your face."

"What's wrong with my face?" I ask, scared now. Perhaps I have been in a terrible fire or a car accident and am permanently disfigured. Perhaps my mother has voluntarily offered me up for plastic surgery without my consent.

"You've really scratched it up," a voice says.

"Don't be ridiculous," I say. "Who did this to me?"

"Well, evidence seems to suggest that you did this to yourself."

"How? When?" I ask, unconvinced.

"Your face was covered in scratches when you came in to check the exam results this morning," I hear the Dean say. "Your eyes were very swollen."

"And then the stinging," I remember. "I couldn't believe my name was there. Was it my name there?"

"The one and only—"

"You seem to be having a marked reaction to stress, but we'd like to do some further assessment," speaks one of the doctors.

"Can I still graduate even if I'm insane? Am I insane?"

The Dean says, "Provided it is your work, you can most certainly graduate. At the top of your class, in fact."

"But what if it isn't my work?"

He asks, "Do you have some concern that it isn't?"

"Well, I mean, what if I am insane and it was the devil or something? Or what if I have a multiple personality disorder and it was some person other than Thelma?"

"Well, that sounds unlikely," says the doctor.

"But I mean legally?" I ask the Dean, seriously concerned. "Legally, if it were some alter ego of mine and not actually Thelma who wrote the exam, could you really allow Thelma to pass?"

"Thelma," interjects my mother. "Have you gone loopy?"

"Stay out of this, Corinna," I chide. "I'm quite serious. I mean, in cases of criminal negligence where an alter ego is thought to have been the perpetrator, the body housing said alter ego is not necessarily convicted. On the basis of that precedent, if my work were to be deemed the product of an alter ego, I would not necessarily pass."

"In light of that kind of reasoning, Thelma, I don't care whether it was the devil within you who wrote that splendid exam. I would pass you with distinction," says the Dean.

"But legally?" I persist.

"I don't know exactly," states the Dean, losing patience.

"But you're the Dean!"

"Perhaps when you're better, you can research it and tell me," he says.

—

There seems to be a lot involved in this assessment. A lot of talking with a lot of different people, and a lot of waiting, and a lot of time wasted in between. I haven't dared look at myself in a mirror—which is a good thing, because the mirrors here are buffed aluminum screwed into the wall, so it wouldn't make a pretty sight even under the best circumstances.

This isn't a psychiatric hospital, I have discovered, but the acute wing of a major hospital. Acute seems to be some code for people who have tried to kill themselves in the past twenty-four hours but have yet to awaken from comas or be assessed and sent off home or to psychiatric hospitals. Like purgatory for nutcases. At least that's as much as I have deduced although no one is telling me a hell of a lot. I am pretty sure I have not tried to kill myself, but then so is the woman in the bed across from me shouting, "I just wanted to see if I could fly." Sure, I do too sometimes, lady, but I do it from the safety of my own bed, not from ten storeys. Sometimes I am grateful for my imagination.

There are a lot of sick individuals here. Most of them are young women. Some of them are wheeling

IVs down the hall and into the elevator and out onto the street to have a cigarette with their IV and a nurse, their gowns open at the back, flapping in the wind. Other people look like they're never planning to leave their beds, some because they're strapped in, others because they've broken their legs, still others because they are overcome by a pill-induced coma or because they simply don't see any reason to move.

People are asking me about my eating and sleeping habits and I seem to be giving them the answers they want to hear, because they are smiling and writing everything down. They are developing a psychological profile, they tell me. And do I hear voices? Well, of course I do, but they're usually coming out of a mouth attached to a face. And do I think people are out to get me? Well, sometimes—because I have good intuition and I'm usually right. And on we go, and I am relieved to learn that they don't think I am capital I Insane, but they think I am reacting to stress and I'd be better off under observation for a week in a hospital.

It's fine, really. It's more peaceful than home and it's not like the last place, where everybody looked all sick and purple-mouthed. I sleep through most of it and leave with a prescription for antidepressants and the name of a therapist and the advice that I take the summer off and relax. I am willing to try the antidepressants but I'm not interested in picking up any orange baseball bats or seeing some therapist who gets confused about whose father we're talking about, so I leave the hospital and bin the piece of paper at the first opportunity.

"Do you think that's wise?" asks Corinna, reaching her hand into the garbage can.

"Look, I don't need that," I assert. "I am perfectly fine. I just want to get on with my life," I say, storming toward the car.

Jesus Blinks

I have won a scholarship to Oxford to do an advanced degree in law. Willy calls me a brainiac and my mother says, "Don't let this go to your head," but secretly I know they are proud, if not somewhat amazed. I am excited about the prospect of going back to England because that's where Heroin, Ginniger and Janawee are, having decided to return several years ago. I remember the message Heroin mimed at me one morning from behind the garden wall: we're not leaving you, we're simply going to live your lives. I am quite sure they have been busy leading the lives I was supposed to live had I not left. Surely I aborted a life in mid-sentence by being whisked away to Canada. Perhaps when I return I can pick up where I left off and lead the life of the clear and confident English woman I was meant to be.

I have always taken comfort in thoughts like these,

all the childlike thoughts you have to make sense of your place in the world. In the thought that the real you is asleep somewhere and you are actually dreaming a life. In the thought that there is a twin of you elsewhere on the planet. In the thought that you are really an adopted child and your parents are out there somewhere, perfect and searching. I have been searching. I am going to England to recover the life that was meant to be mine. I am to be reunited with Janawee, Ginniger and Heroin. I am going to have dinner parties with these three excellent women: Janawee, reunited with her birth family, who is studying piano and riding horses on their farm in the Cotswolds; Ginniger, who is a neurologist conducting experiments on cadavers at Leeds University; and Heroin, who has a feral girl-child strapped to her back and is galloping through Sherwood Forest, trampling snowdrops in search of truth and justice.

—

I live in an old vicarage on Canterbury Road in North Oxford now, the section between Woodstock Road and Walton Street, where the land slopes depressingly toward the Thames. I am not altogether clear about how I came to be here. It was certainly after I left the Magdalen College residence, my first tenancy. I remember feeling OK in the beginning, reassured in my first week by the number of people I met who also thought they were only there as the result of some administrative error. I imagined myself like Jude, staring lovingly at the towers in the distance, an outsider looking in. But Jude never made it this far. His feet stopped with women, the women who embodied his class and his culture and proved to be his millstone. I simply brought the women with me. That is the principal difference. And I came by car.

I might not have been certain who I was, but some kindly porter gave me a key to a room in a quadrangle. Above the door to the room was a name—"Miss T. A. Barley"—what excellent luck, I thought, I'll be sharing a room with Thelma. Miss T. A. Barley also had a little pigeonhole in the Porter's Lodge stuffed full of invitations to mixers with other graduate students in the Middle Common Room, calls to try out for the rowing crew, and requests for donations to support this year's Third World Scholar. I was very impressed by that.

I had a neighbour called Miss N. A. Shepherd who introduced herself to me as such. She said, "It's lovely to meet you, Miss T. A. Barley," and all I could do was stammer out, "Why?"

"Because you appear to be the only other woman in the place," she said. I was about to open my mouth and object and say, "Actually I'm not a woman," but she continued with, "And you know what that means," (which of course I didn't), "it means you don't go traipsing off to the loo in just your stockinged feet," she declared.

I was nevertheless relieved to meet Miss N. A.

Shepherd. I had been disheartened to discover that I
was housed in a corridor of American Rhodes Scholars,
all secretly imagining themselves the next Bill Clinton.
An American drawl shouted "Hey" down the hall as I
struggled with my bags, "are you another Rhodey?" I
hesitated for a moment, flirting with the idea of a
simple, uncomplicated, colluding *Yes*, which would
have made me immediately acceptable on some level,
but said, "Uh, no. Actually, I'm not." There was clearly
no polite question with which to follow this response.
He might have said, "Well, what are you then?" but
instead he said nothing more than "Oh," and disap-
peared into his room never to speak to
me again.

I looked around me in these first few days in Oxford,
walked down narrow streets inhaling diesel fumes, and
noticed how English people don't seem to acknowledge
the presence of anyone else on the street. They walk
removed and withdrawn from others, save for the
embarrassed scuffle as one is inconvenienced by near
collision with another on a sidewalk wide enough for
one only. They don't say excuse me. It's not that they're
rude, it's just that they're defensively preserved somehow, keeping themselves whole and intact. I see myself
in the way they walk, and the concentrated oblivious-
ness of their expressions. I see myself and think,
Maybe this is where I come from. Maybe this is the
way people move in small, tight places. Maybe I am
not a social misfit, I just move in the way English

people move. Maybe I have internalized this sense of space, despite being brought up in the wide, the open, the expanse of Canada. Maybe I am not insane. Maybe it's just that I am English after all.

Among the papers in Miss T. A. Barley's pigeonhole was a small white invitation that said, "Dr. Crispin Stuck has been assigned your 'moral tutor' and requests the pleasure of your company for drinks in his rooms at 6 pm on Sunday of 0th week, Michaelmas, 1992. Regrets only." I was relieved to learn that someone had been appointed to take responsibility for my moral well-being. His (for the guardianship of morality here appeared to be an expressly male domain) primary responsibility, however, seemed to be signing consent forms that declared students fit and responsible (read stable and sane) enough to climb the college tower.

The year before, two students had jumped. Topping yourself seemed to be all the rage. The media had a field day with it: *Oxbridge Blues: High achievers find final solution to relentless pressure to perform at the nation's finest.*

"He was terrifically outgoing and extremely popular with his peers," lamented Mrs. Bosomworth of Tingley Gate, Worcestershire, mother of fresher Timothy, found hanging in his room at Corpus Christi.

Oxford officials declared in their defence that suicide among students at the University was statistically comparable to that among members of the same age group in the general population. Privately, of course, they were a lot more paranoid—hence the consent forms now necessary to climb the tower, and the instruction given to scouts—those staff who cleaned rooms—to report suspected drug use, excessive sleeping or disregard for personal care. On that basis, they should have hauled nearly everyone in, including the tutors.

My moral tutor, Crispin Stuck, undoubtedly thought of depression as some tedious form of self-indulgence—nothing that a couple of brandies couldn't cure. He was expressly flamboyant, a self-proclaimed star in the theatre of life. When I was summoned for drinks just after my arrival, he greeted me at his door with what appeared to be a curtsy, a glass of sherry in his outstretched hand. I think he was expecting a curtsy in return. We weren't taught finishing school etiquette at my high school in downtown Toronto, unfortunately—except if one counts being suspended for writing graffiti on the bathroom walls. (Willy's speciality.)

There were two other new graduate students in Crispin Stuck's room with him, David and Hugh, both young British men, pale, freshly shaven and gawky. David was also studying law, and Hugh, mathematics. I felt distinctly out of place, but fortunately Crispin was there to entertain and demanded nothing more from us than our complete and rapt attention as he took us on a tour of his "collections." He had crammed into his two large rooms more than fifteen harpsichords and virginals, about a dozen gilt-edged mirrors, two enormous chandeliers, and a stuffed deer. It was quite amazing, really. Like the court of some eighteenth-century Viennese aristocrat.

The deer, he told us, was the nemesis of Dr. Pratt, the lately departed proctor of the college. Magdalen College includes a deer park within its extensive grounds, which, Dr. Stuck reported, sheltered at least one deer for every don of the college. When a don died, a deer was killed and consumed at High Table. In this case, Crispin Stuck had killed, stuffed and mounted the deer himself. He performed the deed upon hearing that Dr. Pratt had suffered a heart attack. Much to Crispin's embarrassment, though, Dr. Pratt quickly recuperated in the Radcliffe Infirmary and lived for another year. The white deer named after Crispin was mysteriously poisoned. "Couldn't let it go to waste, though," said Crispin. "Still made a bloody fine Sunday roast," he mused.

—

It was some time after drinks with Crispin that I moved to the vicarage. Six of us live here and I am not altogether sure who is who anymore. I am sometimes not sure if I am me, or Heroin, or the Thelma who has been undergoing a concurrent evolution on this side of the Atlantic, or even, sometimes, my mother. I am not sure if this was her life at age twenty-five and I keep meaning to write to her and ask her. I want to ask her if she ever had a Baby Belling in a bedsit. Ask her if she preferred a madras or a vindaloo. Ask her whether she likes sherry, and whether her shoes used to feel damp in the mornings, or if she knows what a Sloane Ranger is.

We are six women here, six women hiding behind the closed doors of our respective bedsits, making black coffee in the dark. It is dark because we purchase our electricity in fifty pence blocks, and there are only so many fifty pence coins that a girl can accumulate. We are in the dark because it is safer to be here. I pay forty pounds a week in order to hide behind my own door. Forty pounds a week to be safe in the dark.

The woman who first opened the door for me was Lucia. She's a poet who writes painful pieces about love that yields forgiveness in the rain. The kind of yuck that Corinna really goes for. Lucia lives behind the closed door of the bedsit two floors below mine. She opened the door for me and looked me up and down before looking herself up and down, and realized she was buck naked.

"Goodness," she said. "I've even forgotten to put on my shoes."

Her feet were tiny, red and callused. She was tiny, red and callused, blue-veined from top to bottom. She promised me that one day soon we would share a bottle of wine. "I have a bottle, you know," she told me slyly. "I've had a bottle since Christmas." But we have yet to share that bottle. That was two months ago, the day I arrived, and I have caught only fleeting glances of her since. Lucia's taxi driver rings the bell at eight o'clock every morning. I don't know where she goes, but she leaves clutching a handbag overflowing with tiny scraps of paper, and returns home late. I hear her mumbling and scuffling through the corridors in those early morning hours.

There are a lot of noises here, the new noises of a new place that must become familiar before you can ever hope to sleep again. Clare is the noisiest: howling in her sleep, my walls reverberating with her agony. She has metal braces screwed into her legs and takes lithium and smells like sweet sticky vomit all the time. She is afraid to wash her hair and she spends the whole day knitting and unravelling in front of her television. Sometimes I offer her a cup of coffee, but she has never once accepted. In lieu of speech she leaves gifts for me every day, little parcels wrapped in layers of old newspaper—coins, carrots, pieces of chewing gum, or prunes.

We move, for the most part, autonomously in this shared space, each governed by our respective ghosts. This is a halfway house for women between life and somewhere else, and I'm sure, like me, no one knows exactly how she came to be here. Vera tells me she was passing by one day and stopped to stroke the belly of a big orange cat in the front yard of the vicarage. She felt a hand on her shoulder, and she turned and looked up into the strangely gentle but stern face of a weathered old woman who asked her if she needed a place to live.

Mona says that God brought her here. She claims that she and her husband were missionaries in the Philippines in a past life. She paints pictures of tropical vegetation in gaudy primary colours and then photographs them and sticks them askew onto cards. "Only a quid each," she tells me, pressing a stack of fifty into my reluctant hands.

The old woman is Mrs. Morin. At eighty years old, she pushes her bicycle everywhere, and carries the orange cat in a basket at the front. "Oh no, I never *ride* it, my dear," she says to me.

Mrs. Morin and her charges: the five women she must keep safe. We try to keep each other safe. We do not pass judgement here, we are each struggling to create some tiny space in a world that feels alien and hostile. Mrs. Morin, the matriarch, writes long-winded messages for us in her shaky scrawl, and calls us "beloved."

This is a religious house. It was advertised on the church notice board, and I can still hear my mother's friend Pam saying, "Jesus, the girl's got religion." Well, I haven't. But I have started hearing voices. My male-infested residence seemed to be full of voices. I was spending nights at the library just to avoid going back there. I was avoiding sleep because I'd been having a lot of dreams about floating, and rowing crews. On my way home one early morning I collapsed on a bench in a churchyard beside a big and bloody statue of Jesus, and then I noticed a small piece of cardboard tacked to the church's notice board which read: "Room for nice young woman. Forty pounds a week. Electricity extra."

I must have slept on the bench for some time. I awoke abruptly at sunrise as someone across the street threw open the wooden gates to the drive. An old woman, a big bun like a rather solid-looking meringue perched on her head, was thrusting a bicycle aggressively through the gates. She was talking to herself, and muttering banal words of comfort to the mangy calico nestled in a towel in the basket on the front of the bike.

"Good gracious, child, what are you staring at?" she shouted across at me.

"I . . . I was just . . . waiting," I said, startled.

I stared at the cat and she moved to explain.

"Pretty" she said, "is seventeen years old. We are going to the library. We always go to the library." And then, looking at me quizzically, she asked, "Child, what exactly is it you are waiting for? I know you've been out here most of the night. I saw you from my window." She pointed up to the open bay window of the old vicarage.

I looked up and imagined windows full of cats peering into the night through translucent curtains. Creatures saying silent prayers to the God of the small as I rubbed the splinters of Jesus into my back. "It's about the room," I said meekly.

"Goodness," she said, "you should have just rung the doorbell last night instead of camping out here like some homeless urchin!" But then she added more soberly, "*Are* you a homeless urchin, dear?"

I shook my head in embarrassment.

"Well, of course you can have the room," she said. "Look, take my key. I have to leave now, I'm sorry not to be able to show it to you myself, but I do prefer not to have to climb the stairs. Let yourself in and have a look around. I'll let myself in later with the key in the flowerbed."

I had a key. I looked up at this enormous, rambling house almost lost in the greenery that surrounded it. Wisteria wound its way to the upper stories and clematis clung to its brickwork. I opened the gates, shutting them gingerly behind me. It was Lucia who opened the door. Lucia who looked at her veiny, fleshy nakedness, grabbed my hand and pulled me into the foyer, some kind of dumping ground for comings and goings, littered with shoes, ratty jumpers, newspapers and plastic bags stuffed with unknown contents. To the right of the door was a vast post box which spanned the wall from floor to ceiling, pigeon holes for everyone who had ever lived in the house over the course of the last three hundred years. Some of the boxes contained envelopes, others held bicycle lights, slippers and tulip bulbs.

I followed Lucia through a dark narrow hallway, along a threadbare Persian runner covered in cat hair.

At the end of the hallway, a spectacular stained glass window cast a scattering of blue and red triangles over dust-covered books piled high on the floor. Lucia pointed dismissively to her door on the right before we climbed the first staircase. The walls beside us were covered with sepia-stained posters of proverbs and psalms.

On the first floor, Mrs. Morin, Mona and Vera had their respective rooms. The loo, a tiny refurbished closet with a red linoleum floor and shelves labelled with women's names, revealed much; intimacies of the women I had yet to meet. Clare's shelf with its witch hazel, peroxide and shampoo to kill head lice, Vera's with its rich creams, Mona's shelf holding a pumice the size of a football. And Lucia's, with its alarming display reminiscent of a medieval apothecary, its glass jars with rusty lids containing unknown contents. I took comfort in imagining my collection of old toothbrushes and an industrial-size box of Arm and Hammer baking soda on a red shelf, inviting me to scrub my mouth and spit blood into the heavy porcelain sink.

Up the next flight of stairs, the landing was crowded with a refrigerator and a bookshelf full of plates, cutlery, cups, saucers and rusty saucepans. There were two doors. One was mine, she told me, and the other, Clare's. But Clare was "away."

"She will be back," Lucia told me. "She always comes back," she said, smiling sweetly and leaving me to explore what lay behind my new door.

The room was tiny, filthy and dust-covered, but the dust sprang to life and danced in an abundance of sunlight as I entered. From the big bay window overlooking a small balcony I could see Jesus, looking as sad and as sorry as I felt. I collapsed in the brown lumpy bed, which smelled of damp linen, and slept. Slept away the drunken rowing crews, the mixers that turned into gang rapes, and the lecherous professors, sauced in sherry, pickled in posturing, fried like their ugly egg and toast breakfasts.

—

There is a novel by a woman whose name I forget, which Mrs. Morin lends to me. The author describes this place, this vicarage in the nineteen thirties and forties, as a refuge for women, battered women. I know this isn't fiction. I wonder if it isn't Mrs. Morin's story. I wonder if she wrote it. I wonder if I am writing it.

We injure ourselves because of injury. The braces on Clare's legs. I am cautious around her, pretend not to notice her torturous climb up the stairs, pretend not to hear her screaming, pleading to God. But Mrs. Morin wants us to know. She wants us to know that Clare threw herself off a bridge, a bridge not high enough. And she wants Clare to be reminded every day by the braces on her legs.

I am reminded. Clare is howling on the other side of the wall each night and I am dreaming wildly and whispering in the dark. I am whispering:

please don't. please don't pant. this is vomit. this is the

*inside of me thrown out. please don't punish. i cannot
keep my mouth closed and swallow. please don't kiss me
like you love me now. please don't love me in the moment
of killing. i am a hole into which evil comes. i can kill
myself. just kiss me nicely on the forehead and i will spare
you the trouble. just go away and i promise, i promise i
will be good.*

But no, I am not sleeping, I am dreaming again of
the wide, open mouth that sounds like thunder, trying
to inhale the world. I am hovering here, the room long
and narrow below me, my body shrunk to the size of a
twig, a stiff insect clinging to the wall above my pillow.

Sometimes I wonder if I am only playing. Sometimes
I think all roads led me to this place, this house, so I
could play at myself. In the early evenings I crouch low
on the balcony and smoke a cigarette and peek over the
ledge at Jesus crucified. I imagine that he will look up
suddenly and burst out laughing and say, "Hah, fooled
you!" I am afraid to look away, just in case I miss him
blink. When I am writing late at night, I look out to see
him underlit by floodlights. In my life, in this house
where we work so hard to keep ourselves invisible, I
am so conscious that if he were to lift his head just a
little he would see me here, night after night, typing
and twitching, in a place without a forwarding address,
in a world without men, in a world of women and
ghosts. But what if he is the eyes of men? What if all
men see through his eyes? What if my father sees me?
The sight of Jesus scares me now and I pray that those

nails are secure. I draw the blinds and the only reminder of the world is the lingering scent of the presence of other women. We are without words here but I know the others are around me and beneath me, engaged in the harsh battles of their own private wars.

I feel Heroin close in this country and I am speaking to her a lot these days—calling through the trees in the forest, listening to the determined gallop of those hooves, which carry her in circles around me. She is in orbit and she is angry, too angry to stop and speak. I am hurt, but I know somehow that she is on a very important mission and that she cannot slow down and be gentle and known. She is hooves pounding through graveyards, crushing evil bones, trampling human heads that poke like obstinate mushrooms up through her well-worn path. I try not to take it personally, not to feel rejected, but I am, nevertheless, calling out loud in the dust she kicks up in her passing.

Aubrietia

Miss N. A. Shepherd says, "It's a damn sight better than that stinking locker room." She is my guest for tea on a cold and wet October Saturday afternoon. She has just broken up with Luke the Pluke from Cambridge, and she's on a real downer.

"I hate that bloody drive," Naomi says. "I'm glad I won't have to do *that* anymore. I have to entertain myself when I'm driving by imagining extraordinary lives for the people in other cars. Pathetic! Most of the cars I pass are driven by really reptilian businessmen types, the sort who have forced my opinion of men to an all-time low. They all drive the same type of car and dominate the road as if that mostly shrivelled one inch of bodily fluid-evacuating flesh hanging between their thighs gives them the right to treat all other human life as an unnecessary inconvenience. I imagine their sterile spiritual lives and it keeps me amused for hours." She pauses. "Do you know what I mean?"

We have had this discussion before. The one wherein I ask Naomi, "If you think they're all such pigs, why do you sleep with them?"

She usually refers to some awesome power beyond her control. "Some primordial instinct. Some chemical thing," explanations I can digest more easily than, "Because it can be so great," or "Because I love him."

She is determined to hand me the key to this awesome power. We have been once to the night club on the Oxpens Road where we drank our half pints of bitter and hugged a post and Naomi ogled a group of American marines. She has bought me a pair of black leggings from Marks and Spencer, tweezed my eyebrows mercilessly and showered me in White Musk from The Body Shop. We burn aromatic oils in my room, which is supposed to "put you in the mood."

"What mood?" I keep asking her.

"You'll know it when you feel it," she says assuredly. "Starts in your fanny and works its way up."

"Nom!" I object.

I have tried to resist this fashion/lifestyle make-over by saying, "But really, I think that's tacky," on more than one occasion, but then yield to her insistence that I have a hair rethink. I have had my legs ruthlessly waxed, yet this chemical thing shows no evidence of surfacing. I am a piece of wet driftwood refusing to light.

Then this happens. Naomi comes to pick me up at the Bodleian Library one evening and we go to Rajiv Ali's on the Cowley Road for a curry. We sometimes do. I have a biryani and she has a vindaloo and we share some pappadums and pickle and an order of saag aloo and I say:

"Did I ever tell you about . . . "

And she interjects with "Suresh?" but indulges me and laughs and quickly adds, "No, who is he?"

At some later juncture she brings me back with, "Your point being, Suresh made a wicked curry."

"My point being—ugh—Nom—can't you see?"

"I know, Thelma, he shook your world."

"Well, yeah. I mean it was as if he was sent there to teach us something."

"Mmm, hmm,"

"No, I'm serious, Naomi."

"I know," she says reassuringly. "But check out this bloke," she says, rolling her eyes in the direction of the man seated to her left at the adjacent table.

I take a peek and say, "Yeah, what about him?"

"I think he fancies you."

"Don't be ridiculous," I scoff. "Men don't fancy me."

"He's given you the once-over at least ten times," she nods.

"Naomi, men don't check me out."

"Sure they do. And this guy is, shamelessly."

I am never sure what to do in these situations. If I

were my mother I'd probably thrust out my new C cups. If I were Naomi I'd probably shout across the table at the end of the night, "Right, then. Are you coming home with me or not?" (Which she actually does, some months later, to a stranger in a crowded pub who eventually becomes her husband.) But apart from these two role models I have little to go on, so I steal a few surreptitious glances. He is pale and thin and deeply engaged in conversation with the man seated opposite him. He is leaning forward, arms crossed on the table, now reaching across to pull a Silk Cut from his dinner companion's cigarette pack, nodding his head and periodically pushing his wire-rimmed glasses up the bridge of his nose.

"This is what we do," says Naomi, pulling a pen from her bag and turning over her napkin. "We write him a note."

"We don't," I whisper in disbelief.

"Sure we do."

"Have you ever done this?" I ask, uncertain.

"'Course," she says. "Plenty of times."

"And does it ever work?"

"Depends what you mean by work. So he may or may not respond—but the beauty of this is, he takes the note, he is invariably flattered and then he does with it what he will. You never even have to know if you've been rejected. You never have to see the bloke again, and if he doesn't call, you just tell yourself that his gay lover burned the number when he found it in the pocket of his jeans while doing the laundry. Nothing ventured, Thelma."

"No, this guy doesn't have a lover," I say.

"Intuition?" Naomi asks.

"He's missing something," I say.

"Well, then," she glares at me, wide-eyed.

———

I am going on a date. Oh my God. Jesus God, why the hell am I doing this? I would rather be at home studying, I would rather be at the Bodleian, I would rather be anywhere but here on Little Clarendon Street in squeaky new black shoes walking toward Café Tryst. Naomi is watching me from the other end of the street calling, "Thelma, I'll kill you if you don't do this." A brief moment passes where I do think, "That's OK, I'd rather be dead."

He is there, tapping his pack of Silk Cuts nervously on the mahogany bar. His legs are wrapped and wrapped again around the legs of a stool. His thumb is poised on his lower lip. I am Patrick, he is Thelma . . . I mean, he is Patrick, I am Thelma.

"I am Thelma. I am pleased to meet you. I'll have orange juice. Thank you very much."

"I don't drink either," he says. "At least I try not to. Alcohol's a depressant. Silk Cut?" he offers. "I'm trying to quit myself," he says, shaking his head.

"Thank you," I say, a little alarmed by the look of my

nails pulling at a cigarette, unfamiliar but not altogether displeasing after the manicure Naomi has
insisted upon.

"I wasn't going to phone," he says. "But I was
carrying your number around in my pocket and it
started to feel heavy there. I was working in the rain,
on the roof of my house, and I could feel this napkin in
my pocket. I got soaked through and I pulled out the
note but it was wet and the numbers were starting to
blur." Patrick pats his pocket like he's feeling for a pet
rock. "More rain and I would have lost the numbers
altogether."

I am imagining a blue river of numbers. I am
imagining a sea of missed opportunities and faded
promises. I am imagining Patrick building a roof in the
rain.

"You'd be better off building an ark," I say. We talk
weather for slightly too long and retreat into silence.

"Are you sure you won't join me in a glass of wine?"
he asks.

I am thinking about this literally. Join you in there?
Swim with you to the Antipodes? Float like flotsam on
the Pacific? Drown like a slug in tequila, preserved,
immortalized and potent?

"Thanks," I say.

"I try not to. Like I said, it's a depressant."

"Do you get depressed then?" I inquire politely, as
prompted.

"I've been depressed for the last seventeen years," he

says. "Chronic, low-level. Feeling like I walk in the margins of life. Everything just slightly off-colour."

"That's wonderful," I exclaim enthusiastically.

"Wonderful?"

"Well, not wonderful that you should feel that way, but refreshing to hear that you know what it feels like," I explain.

"Well, I had suspected you felt similarly," he says.

"What made you think that?"

He is good enough not to suggest the obvious—a thousand immediately observable neuroses—and says, "I thought that's what you'd picked up from me. Why you'd written."

"I don't know why I wrote, " I think aloud. "I've never done that before."

"Well, I'm glad you did," he says, smiling at me.

—

We are moving in each other's shadows, taking delicate steps at fifty-degree angles, peering out occasionally to catch the sun in each other's hair. It involves talking into the early hours of the morning on benches outside pubs after closing. Holding hands and speaking softly and sharing little details hitherto housed in a bulging file of secrets. It is lovely and I am becoming braver. I think this man is my boyfriend. I think I am in something called a relationship. It is hard for me to know if I am, because I do not know what one is supposed to feel like. I realize this is what it must be, but perhaps there are just not enough words in English to describe this kind of arrangement. Arrangement. As if it has order, a structure somehow.

I call him on the phone and ride my bike to his house in east Oxford on sunny afternoons in the spring. Sitting in his garden, he tells me he planted aubrietia because it reminds him of me—hugging the ground and beautiful. I have never been beautiful before. He is making tea and toast and soft-boiled eggs and he is asking me to live with him. He is forty-one years old and doesn't want to live alone any longer. He wants to share this house. He wants to love me. He holds my hands in his and I like the feel of his hands. I stare at them all the time, marvelling that they are real, that they have built houses and that they want to hold my face. I like leaning my forehead against his chest—the hardness of his breastbone and his heart beating close to the surface. I like the smell of him through his shirt. I feel fragile and hesitant, but not afraid. Small and slow-moving, but not stopping. He wants to make love to me, but he fears it. He fears the pain, to cause it, but also to feel it. He finds sex very painful, he tells me. And because he knows pain and because he is as afraid as I am, this talk does not frighten me. He knows sex can kill. He needs to hold my hand all the way to the doctor's. And hold my hand all the way home. And hide with me there in the dark and quiet after his circumcision, where he feels embarrassment, shame and pain, and I feel gentle, giving.

—

I am sitting quietly with Patrick on the grey carpet, watching first division football on the TV. He is trying not to drink much.

We are sleeping side by side now, my head in his armpit, listening to the sounds a man makes in his sleep. The sounds are unfamiliar but I feel ready to hear them, ready to listen.

He is getting better, pulling on his Levi's and smiling now. Getting ready for football practice and lacing up his shoes. Saying: Let's get a really good bottle of wine and go down to the river later. I think I might have liked it better when we were quiet though, because I can feel the effort involved in my smile. It's not coming naturally like it was only two weeks ago. What's coming naturally now is a familiar fear, which creeps up from my feet to my face. He is telling me he can hardly wait to make love to me and I am thinking, If only I could have an operation, too. If only I could rest for a time in quiet pain and awaken new and willing. He is looking forward and I am closing inward. He is thinking of oceans, swimming, and freedom, while I am thinking of twigs and rocks and the rotten, hollow carcasses of trees.

I am waking from a terrible dream where I am being crushed between the jaws of a faceless, dying monster, a dragon consuming human lives in order to sustain its existence. My body is pinned down and my lungs are collapsing. Patrick is on top of me and I have stopped breathing. My ribs have been crushed and my lungs deflated, but blood is coursing through me, spinning through my head. Every inch of me is observable heartbeat. "I think I am dying," is all I can manage to get out.

"Oh sweetheart, I was just hugging you," says Patrick gently. "It just feels good to be this close to you."

But I know this is not right. I feel him hard and wanting and I am confused. *Are you lying, Patrick? To love me like this is to kill me. This is how love feels.*

I am enlisting Heroin's support. I am summoning the army of her with my thoughts and she is galloping on her white horse through gardens in east Oxford, ploughing through vegetable patches and ripping up flowerbeds, leaping fences and kicking up a massive great cloud of dark soil. The cloud is hanging there, low over the garden and Patrick says, "What can we do about it? It's so ominous. Can't we make it go away?" But I know he cannot say the right thing and make it retreat, he can only say the wrong thing and bring it closer. And closer and closer it comes.

Limited Options in the Late Twentieth Century

Sleep is no longer an option. There are fewer and fewer options altogether. Crispin Stuck won't give me permission to climb the tower and none of the bridges in Oxford are quite high enough. There is Port Meadow where I could lie in the grass like Lewis Carroll and dream of Alice and pray that the horses and cows would run over my hidden, prostrate body. If it were a century earlier I could commit a heinous crime and be shipped to Australia and hope that a storm would cast me into homicidal waters. There was the twelve gauge my father used to have in the house that was never really a house and certainly never a home in the country.

I am worried that he sees me. I am worried that he lives in other men's eyes and that he is looking through the eyes of that Jesus on Canterbury Road, following me. Sometimes I see him, a tiny speck in Patrick's irises, and I am terrified. Although Patrick is much bigger, he has no idea that another man is lurking in his eyeball, waiting for a moment to strike out. I am on guard. I do not sleep now. I watch Patrick's face while he dreams and I feel like I am in terrible danger. I have it in mind that I will have to secure Jesus on the crucifix with a few more nails. I will do it at night, I will use thick screws and I will chisel out his eyes.

There is the medicine cabinet. It strikes me that it is the only option of this time and place because I cannot find a bridge, or a ship on cruel waters, or a herd willing to trample me, or a gun, and I cannot wire a car, or make myself worth being murdered, and Jesus can be resurrected. But I do know how to swallow. I've had years of practice.

BOOK 2

Out-of-body Privileges

I've thrown my bed out. It's lumpy and it moves on wheels while I toss pennies in my sleep. I have only the mattress now, one side wedged into the inches between the radiator and the floor. This is where I am—pinned in the remotest corner of a psychiatric hospital where I read, eat, smoke, drink tea, write and twitch late into each night. But not sleep. I don't sleep here. I haven't slept for weeks. I have stopped lying down. I am afraid of the dreaming. I sit instead with my back roasting against the radiator. Hard brown stripes run parallel to my spine, and my thighs have bruises caused by the rough hands of men in dreams.

It is not proper dreaming, because I am not asleep. I am awake, semi-conscious, levitating, dreaming about a mouth loud and bloody, seething, tearing the stitches that can no longer bind it closed. I rise up, up above it, stapled to the wall here, like a little leech looking down on the world over a huge bed, which grows wider and wider and longer and touches the frame of the door.

There are different rooms that can look virtually the same from this perspective. There are different nights, and different years—and though the images are always the same, they are nonetheless frightening, they are creatures that can never be tamed. I have been dreaming this dream continuously and to be awake and to be alive is simply to distract me from its buzz, hum, suspension.

I am snapped back away from it, sweating because it is the witching hour and Poppy is plodding through a waltz on the old piano. Poppy's playing kills dreams. Kills mine, but catapults Clare into the open arms of the devil. Clare is here screaming thickly, the sound bubbling its way through blood. I couldn't hear her this clearly when she lived down the hall from me in the vicarage on Canterbury Road. But when I came here, she told me. She limped toward me, blue haired and wild-eyed, and said, "I put you here."

"This has nothing to do with you," I told her.

But she repeated, "I put you here. It was all those times I called you CUNT when you walked by me in the hall. I was screaming CUNT at you."

"Clare," I objected, "I never heard you say that." She walked by me then, blankly, through the garden toward the dirt in the dead flowerbed of February.

I tell myself that my being here has nothing to do with her, but I am not certain. Maybe she speaks another language, a dialect that I don't understand consciously but one I can nevertheless hear with something other than my ears. Now I hear cunt all the time. I see cunt, I feel cunt, I smell cunt, I am cunt.

My door is open to a constant stream of traffic. The fuckers coming. Coming to fuck, fucking to come. Names beginning with the letter D. Damian and Dave and Dangerous and Dick. One long endless semi-conscious dream about fucking—fucking a mouth that is trying to inhale the world, sucking.

—

Smartie time. That's what Sasha in the lineup in front of me calls it. Temazepam and Haloperidol. I love it, boxing the air around me, determined to stand up. I can fight as hard as I can, my mind and my body flying, punching, racing, going nowhere—you could blow me over in one short breath. "It's time for bed, Thelma," a white voice speaks from somewhere. But I am loving the sound of my own voice, loving the way everything rhymes, but my lips, my lips are no longer moving, and my feet, they've been lifted from the floor. I am being carried like a piece of firewood, about to be thrown into the flames rising from my bed. I will not lie down. I am sure that if I lie down I will burn here. By the cold light of morning I will be nothing but a grey log that has retained its shape, and when they shake me, I will crumble into ashes.

I sleep, drugged, diseased, deceased. I burn and crumble and rise again like a phoenix. I am not well, they tell me. Have I always been not well? Have I always been what they tell me? I have only my journal to go by, but I am sure other people have been writing in it. There are passages here by people I don't know. There is a lot of bad writing. I know I haven't always lived here, but the only places I am willing to remember are the ones twelve paces away or less.

There are women here who cannot remember their names or which room they live in. They have an eerie calm dullness about them. They get electroshocked. I never want to get electroshocked because then you forget where you are and then you really are crazy. I do not remember the past but I do remember the tiny things right in my face. There is a way to make a map of Canada by connecting the cracks in the ceiling, there is a way to the bathroom, there is a way to make Ovaltine and there is a way out of this place. Ultimately, though, whether it's your past or your present that you forget, it is the forgetting that sustains you. This is a world of limited options, a world without knives and forks. Remembering to forget is the only option left.

—

One morning I wake up and look in the shiny piece of tin they call a mirror here. I look and I look and try to pry apart this face.

"Is that you?" I whisper.

"Where the fuck have you been?" the face says back to me.

"I've been here the whole time!" I spit back. "Where the fuck have you been?"

That was the moment we got reacquainted—me and my face. Up until then I'd been too afraid to look into this thing they called a mirror because there'd be some woman there going "blah blah blah," and I didn't know what the fuck she was on about. I would just brush my teeth, spit blood and hurry out of there.

After that I started asking if I could go outside. A nurse came with me at first and we would sit in silence on a bench, have a smoke and stare at nothing. Then I started feeding the squirrels. I fed them Fruit Loops that I got from the kitchen staff. I thought they looked pretty there, all pink and yellow and orange and plastic-looking, scattered on the snow. One day I made snow angels like I used to when I was little in the front yard on Merton Street. After that they let me go outside alone.

———

I was trying to concentrate. It was Mastermind and I knew all the answers, but people were making so much noise and walking in front of the television and I was getting really angry. There was this new woman, Leona, and she was just flipping out—swearing her head off, pelting out words like an automatic rifle in about a million different languages. She threw herself on the floor and writhed about, shouting, "Fuck me, suck me, chuck me, yuck me," shoving her pelvis up to the sky.

And then I lost it. I leapt out of my chair and I screamed at her, "Shut up, you vain bitch, nobody wants to fuck you!"

"Hey!" White coat said, grabbing my arm and pulling me into the corner of the room. "She's not well," he said gravely.

"She's fucked!" I shouted at him. "She's a fucking nymphomaniac!"

"She's just not well," he said again.

"Well, if not well is just a big euphemism for being a fucking nymphomaniac, then OK! She's not well! I just wish she'd shut up!"

I didn't really believe that, about "not well" meaning you're a nymphomaniac. I was angry, and what he said scared me. Is that what "not well" looks like? Is that what I look like when I'm not well? And why did he say it to me? Does that mean I'm supposed to know the difference now—does that mean I am no longer not well?

It's true, I have started washing my hair now. I've even found an old trashy lipstick in the bottom of my duffle bag, covered in lint and tobacco, but I put some on anyway, yesterday, before I went out for a walk. The nurse at the door gushed at me, "Don't you look pretty. Lipstick. You must be feeling better." I told her to bugger off. That's what she deserves for being such a patronizing bitch.

I was sorry for saying it. I felt really embarrassed. I never know what to say when someone says something nice to me. When I noticed her sitting by the door again today, I put my lipstick on again before I went out. She didn't say anything to me this time, and I was secretly disappointed. I waited a moment and then turned around in the hallway and came back and said, "Marjorie, I'm going to get myself a cup of tea. Can I bring you one?"

"No thanks, Thelma," she said, but then she hesitated. "Well, all right then," and held out her cup. I held her cup between my hands. I held it hard, grateful for the feel of it, for the tangible evidence of a world outside myself.

But the Greatest of These is Love

Crispin Stuck, my moral tutor, was surprisingly kind to me. He visited twice and brought me a bag of plums and told me that when he was an undergraduate they used to refer to this place as Warneford College. He generously widened the scope of the University to include the local psychiatric hospital and made me feel as if I was simply on loan to one of the other colleges for the rest of the term: Oxford's forty-fifth college, with a better pool table than any of the other junior common rooms. Crispin played pool with me there and confided, when I won the game, that he'd fallen in love with an undergraduate to whom he'd offered a plum at Parson's Pleasure the summer before and his nerves had been shot since. I let him win the next game.

Naomi came to visit me every day. At first she had her worried face, but increasingly she became the amusing and not altogether politically-correct self I knew and loved. She moved from: "You know you could have told us if you felt anyone was pressuring you—me, Patrick, the school" to:

"That Poppy, now she's interminably doolally."

Patrick came every afternoon but never stayed long. He was a little bit of everything—sad, disappointed, hurt, angry. I felt guilty for having wolfed down his six-months' supply of Prozac, and told him I would pay to replace it.

"That's not the point, Thelma," he said. "I promised myself this would never happen," he said sadly.

"But that was never your job," I told him.

—

"I think you need a break, Thelma," he says the next day.

"From what?"

"From me. From this place. Take the pressure off. Take some time off."

"To do what?" I ask helplessly.

"Exorcise those demons. Find a decent therapist."

"But I'm fine now," I plead. "I've got my course to finish."

"Your course can wait," he says. "You can take a term off. Two terms. A leave of absence. It's not uncommon. I checked it out with Dr. Stuck," he states.

"You what?"

"I secured you a leave of absence."

"You what?" I repeat helplessly, feeling everything slipping away from me. "But what about my work?"

"It's just a leave of absence. You can come back when you're ready and pick up where you left off."

"Come back from where?" I plead. "Don't do this," I beg. "Don't get rid of me, Patrick. Please."

"Your mother thinks you'd be better off at home."

"My mother?" I stammer. "You've been talking to my mother?"

"I'm not getting rid of you, Thelma, I just want what's best for you."

"My mother?" I ask, panicked now.

"I didn't know what to do. I felt helpless. There's nothing I can do," says Patrick. "I thought your mother might know. I thought maybe you had done this before and she'd know what to do."

"She knows nothing," I say spitefully through my tears, but my voice and the world around me are fading.

"She knows nothing," I repeat in a whisper.

Dreamy Spacecake

I am apparently going to a place called home. Home. Home? I thought this was home. I thought this was supposed to be my home. There is no home, but here I am rattling with drugs, getting off a plane at Pearson Airport, hugging a bag full of case studies.

"Thelma," I hear my mother's voice call out.

I paste on a stony smile that smacks of trying to look perfectly all right and say, "Corinna. You didn't have to meet me. I could have taken a taxi."

"Don't be stupid, Thelma. You're not well," she says.

"I am perfectly fine," I protest, tight-lipped.

"You're fat!" she exclaims. "I expected to see you wasted away to nothing, but you're fat."

"I'm not fat, mother!" I scream. "It's just this fucking lithium!" I yell out so that mothers hugging daughters smelling like airplanes, and lovers kissing lovers once separated by miles, are looking over their shoulders in curiosity.

"Thelma, keep your voice down," she says, embarrassed. "Have you lost your mind?" she chides.

"Oh, that's really helpful, Mum. Nice," I snip. "What the fuck am I doing here?" I say aloud to myself.

"I'm glad you're fat," says Corinna, leading me by the arm toward the doors that go whoosh, a big blast of cold air, and the cigarette smoke of those banished outdoors sweeping in.

"I'm not fat," I say with clenched teeth. "And I'm not a fucking invalid," I say, wrenching my arm out of her grip. "You're fat," I say in a feeble attempt at revenge.

"Thelma!" she says looking hurt. "I will forgive you only because I know you're not in your right mind."

"So I'm in my left mind? Or the wrong mind? Or someone else's mind?"

"You're not making any sense, Thelma," she says, exasperated.

———

"But we don't live here," I protest. "We don't live in the suburbs."

I am incredulous. This is not our house. These are not trees.

"We do now," says my mother quietly. "I've moved in with Warren," she starts to explain.

"Warren the dentist?" I ask. "Mum, you're taking this North American thing way too far. That's not a house,"

I say, pointing at the bungalow sprawling horizontally across perfect grass.

"Well, I like it, Thelma," she defends.

"But it's Warren's," I exclaim.

"And I'm very happy here," she says. "And Warren wants you to feel it's your home, too."

"I'll find a hotel," I say quite seriously.

"Don't be ridiculous, Thelma. You're not well."

"Would you stop saying that!" I yell. "I am perfectly fine. And if I wasn't, this sure wouldn't help."

"Still as ungrateful as ever," my mother sighs.

"Oh fuck off."

"I'm ignoring that," says my mother, getting out of the car.

——

Warren is making lentil soup, which he knows is my favourite. He's not English but he might as well be, since he is only capable of expressing affection through food. He must be thinking soup is what you feed a sick person. He's a scientist, for Christ's sake, and he's feeding lentil soup to a mentally ill person in hope of a cure.

I have to admit, though, he has been remarkably nice to me. What is even more remarkable perhaps is that I have let him. He has driven me to the psychiatrist's office and taken me to Just Desserts for coffee afterwards. We have sat together in the smoky, booming space and he has told me that he knows what it feels like. In fact, the first time he brings it up I am not sure I've even heard him correctly. He raises his voice so I can hear him over the music and he yells out, "Until Prozac," just as the music stops. Everybody turns around. Warren is embarrassed but I'm sure they're all nodding, "you too, huh."

I don't like my psychiatrist. He says things like, "I would probably diagnose you as having a borderline personality disorder," and I have done enough reading to know that he regards me as a manipulative incurable piece of trash for the psychiatric waste bin.

I shout at him. "Look. I don't find that very helpful! I don't need another label stamped across my forehead."

Which leads him to say, "What's wrong with your face anyway—your skin?" which is another thing I don't need to hear, and I burst into tears. I thought the scars were virtually invisible after all the vitamin E.

"That's so sexist," I say. "What about my face? I thought you were supposed to be analyzing my mind."

He tells me that my anger is transference and I want to tell him to fuck the hell off. I'll be the first to admit I have a problem with men, but this guy is an authentic sexist bastard in his own right. Fuck transference.

"I think I need to see a woman," I say.

"Suit yourself," he says, flipping through his rolodex until he finds Dr. Ruth Novak—clinical psychologist and psychoanalyst.

———

I am in the waiting room. Beige. No bean bag chairs or orange baseball bats here. I guess you can give up the props when you're charging a million dollars an hour. I do not shake her hand. Remembering Lydia Hutchinson's outstretched arms, I want to make it clear from the start that I am not one for touching. We are very civilized, sitting across from one another in square beige leather chairs. She is all red. Red lips and red hair and red nails and a red jacket. A short black skirt and pointy patent leather shoes. She is tiny and perfectly manicured. I feel large and slovenly by comparison. This will never work, I think immediately. You are too little and I am afraid I will break you. You are too perfect. I am too damaged.

She is silent and I am silent. She is perched on the edge of her chair, looking very eager and attentive, and she is intimidating me. What am I supposed to say? Normally people like this say, "How are you feeling and are you eating and are you sleeping or not sleeping and are you taking your medication and here's your prescription and I'll see you in two weeks." But she is saying nothing.

"Why don't you ask me something?" I prompt.

"Why don't you tell me why you're here," she says.

"Because a few years ago I ended up in hospital because I had stopped eating, and then a couple of years later I ended up in hospital again because I had tried to scratch my eyes out and then recently I ended up in hospital again because I took a drug overdose."

"Why?"

"Because first they thought I had anorexia, and then

they told me I had manic depression and now they think I have a borderline personality disorder."

"And what do you think?"

"I think I'm fucked up."

"Does the medication help you?"

"I don't think so," I say. "I still want to die."

"Well, why don't you stop taking it," she suggests.

I feel my heart begin to beat faster. This is something very very different, but I do not know what it is. Finally I say:

"Because maybe I'll kill myself."

"But you said the medication doesn't take away the feeling of wanting to die."

"No," I say. "But maybe it stops me from actually doing it. I don't know." I shrug.

"Well, you could hold on to me instead," she says plainly.

My heart skips a beat. "What do you mean?" I ask, suspicious.

"I mean if you feel like killing yourself, you can tell me. We'll get through it together."

"You can't do that," I stammer.

"Why not?"

"You can't take responsibility for someone's life like that."

"But I'm prepared to," she says

"How can you say that?" I question. "You don't even know me."

"But I want to," she says.

This is all too much for me. *You what?* I think. *How
dare you? You can't touch me. How dare you go straight
for the jugular. Get away from me. I will not feel or yield
to you.* And she is asking me to promise her that I will
not try to kill myself, but I cannot make that promise—
I feel like it is the only option I have left, and if it is
taken away from me then I will have no control at all.

—

I am becoming a dreamy spacecake. I take the subway
home to the bungalow in the suburbs, close my door
and stare at the ceiling. Act like a teenager, mouthing
the words to Sarah McLachlan and Shawn Colvin.
Falling in love. Being treated like a teenager.

Corinna asks, "Thelma, what is it with you now? Are
you taking drugs?"

I answer snidely, "Uh, yeah. As a matter of fact, I
am. Lithium, valproic acid, fluoxetine and paroxetine,
nefazodone when I feel paranoid and trazodone when I
can't sleep. All of them, I do believe, covered under
Warren's drug plan."

"I mean illegal drugs, Thelma," she snips.

"Well, I've never known you to have a problem with
illegal drugs before," I quip, referring to the days with
Suresh, now conveniently erased from her memory.

"Keep your voice down, Thelma," she says.

Oops—history gets rewritten with a new relationship
and there are things Warren doesn't know.

—

I am staring into a bowl of lentil soup. "It's just as good

as it always is, Warren," I reassure him. "I'm just not all that hungry."

"A new love, perhaps?" He smiles at me.

"Don't be ridiculous," my mother scoffs.

Behind closed doors I am swooning again. Writing poetry, tearing up paper for collages. I am covered in glue-stick and brimming with words. As a matter of fact, I'm not taking drugs, I say to myself, and dump out the contents of my sock drawer into a garbage bag. Enough drugs here for a Jonestown massacre and although I am resigning myself not to take them, I am not yet willing to let them out of my sight. I put the first package in an envelope and address it to Dr. Novak.

Cave Dwellers

I have decided that if I have to exist on earth then I will do so as a rock inhabiting the same cave as Dr. N. We can whisper and write messages to each other with matches in the dark. I have found a rock in the ravine that I think quite resembles me and I have given it to Dr. N. for safekeeping. We are weeks into this and still she says very little and I say even less. But my whole world is nevertheless about her. I am interested in nothing but sleeping in the interstices, daydreaming my way through subway rides and instant tellers and Corinna's blahdy blahdy blah.

"An Item"

Patrick has come to visit. My mother is outrageously flirtatious and Warren doesn't seem the least bit threatened and they all seem to be enjoying it, only I wish to be left alone to daydream and sleep with the rock that I have borrowed back from Dr. N. for the duration of Patrick's visit. He thinks the rock is funny. "Therapist stoned to death by flying transitional object," is his favourite joke now, and although I know he is not being malicious, I regret having told him.

He sleeps in my bed with me but I feel like a rigid twig next to him and if it weren't for the fact that I fear Corinna wilting at the thought of losing the only son-in-law she might ever have, I would tiptoe away and sleep on the couch. I am losing him. He is my friend and my brother, gentle and supportive, and I am in love with someone else. I am in love for the first time in a way I would willingly give myself to, physically. I am dismantled, I am liquid, I am in search of flight, of merger. I am resident in utero. No part of me lives outside anymore and I am incapable of even touching Patrick's hands.

"You're not coming back, are you, Thelma," he asks me sadly at the airport.

"I can't leave," I say helplessly.

"I want what's best for you," he says. "I thought you'd be better here for a while, but I didn't think I was letting you go forever."

"Oh God," is all I can manage.

"It's so sad," he says.

"I'm too young for you," I offer. He turns his head away in an effort to hide the unfamiliar sight of tears falling from an English face.

—

But I am too young. I am only four years old. And I am busy living in transference land with Dr. N. as my new mother, Mummy Roo. We live together in a spotless white house of hardwood floors and blue linen curtains and mottled marigolds in boxes on the windowsills. We have a big orange boy-cat named Teddy and a garden full of vegetables and cornflowers and cosmos and a tortoise named Roger who lives amongst the lettuces. Mummy Roo does a lot of baking and generally a lot of comfort-food making while I sit at a big round pine table copying new words into a lined notebook. "Teach me a new word," I say to her without looking up from my book, and she says "Um. OK. How about bliss?"

It is not always a happy domestic arrangement, though. I get fractious and impatient and occasionally she is tired and a little bit irritable. We don't fight, but for not fighting I seem to do an awful lot of yelling and crying. Sometimes she comes home tired from work and all I want to do is play and splash the bathwater but she tells me to hurry up because she has to go out and teach her class at 7:30 and the babysitter has arrived.

We continue in this day-to-day way for months, but then things start to go wrong. She is going to teach on a Thursday and I know Tuesday nights are her teaching nights. And I know she doesn't usually wear her black dress and gold necklace for teaching. And this time Karen the babysitter isn't coming, I'm going to Mummy Roo's sister Liza's, and I'm spending the night there with my cousin Jilly the girlie-girl who is nine years old and a priss.

I am throwing a temper tantrum. Mummy Roo is trying to lift me from the floor, but I am clutching the white carpet in my little fists, screaming, "I'm not going!" Somehow she manages to zip up my snowsuit over my hysterical heaving body and latch me into the passenger seat of the car. I am blubbering, my back pinned against Aunty Liza's knees and her hands on my shoulders as Mummy Roo pulls the front door of Liza's house closed. I am sure I am never going to see her again.

Aunty Liza is making potato latkes for dinner

because she knows I love them, but I am ignoring her as she says, "Honey, come on over here and help me." I am crouched in the corner, still in my snowsuit, with my knees pulled to my chest. I am closing my eyes and wishing myself into a stone, inhaling my limbs. I am resolving never to move again.

At some point I fall asleep there. When I wake up I am wearing one of Jilly the girlie-girl's nightgowns and I am in bed, Jilly snoring like she is inhaling cupcakes beside me. I sit upright, panicked, and get out of bed and go into the hallway.

"Mummy," I call out. "Mummy!" I shout in desperation.

Liza emerges in her fuzzy blue slippers, without her glasses, saying, "What is it, Thelma, can't you sleep?"

"Mummy," is all I can manage to whimper. "I want Mummy Roo."

"Oh sweet," says Aunty Liza. "She'll be here in the morning, Thelma. I promise," she reassures me.

But it's not good enough. I am determined to get back into my snowsuit. Liza is fighting me all the way. Jilly pokes her head out of her bedroom doorway to see what all the fuss is about, and says, "She's such a baby."

"I am not!"

"Jilly, go back to bed," Liza chastises. "You're not helping."

Jilly tells me to "take a pill" and skulks off.

Liza carries me to the kitchen and plonks me down

in the middle of the kitchen table because I refuse to uncross my legs. "What'll it be?" she asks.

"What?" I ask through a face full of tears.

"Chocolate or caramel?" she asks. But I'm still confused. "Ice cream. Chocolate or caramel?" she asks again, but I don't answer. "Well, I'm having chocolate," she says, opening the freezer door.

"Move over," she says and comes to sit beside me on the table. I am confused. Grown-ups don't sit on the table and eat chocolate ice cream. "Wanna bite?" she asks, waving a spoon in front of my face. I shake my head. "Didn't your Mum ever do this when you were a baby?" she says, flying her spoon through the air. I shake my head again. "Didn't she ever pretend it was an airplane?" she asks.

"Hale-Bopp comet," I say quietly.

"Pardon?" asks Liza, looking at me.

"Pretend it's Hale-Bopp comet," I repeat.

"Will you eat it if I do?" asks Liza hopefully.

—

My eyes have just stopped hurting from all the crying, and things are just starting to get back to normal, when it is Thursday again. If I just pretend that it's not Thursday, maybe Mummy Roo will forget it is, too. But no. Here she is home, being extra specially nice to me and I am suspicious. I refuse to take my bath until she has changed into her blue dress. Then I refuse to get out of the bath. She is trying to pull the plug but I am threatening to bite her.

"Thelma," she is saying, "your behaviour is so aggressive."

So I stand up and jump into her arms and shriek, "I'm out!" soaking her blue dress and her shiny red hair. "I'm out, Mummy!" I shout again.

"That's good, Thelma," she says, but she is obviously distressed. She is flicking the hangers in her closet again, asking me, "This one?" about the yellow and black one.

I shake my head and say, "No, it's ugly."

"Well, how about this one?" she says, pulling out the red one.

"No," I say. "It's stinky."

"Well, I think it's pretty," she says, and starts to pull the blue one over her head.

"No!" I shout. "It's ugly!" and I am off again, gripping little fistfuls of carpet and crying, but she appears to be ignoring me.

"Thelma," she says seriously after a couple of minutes. "Sweetheart, can I talk to you? Can you just calm down a minute so I can talk to you? Look," she says, lifting me off the floor onto her bed. "There's nothing to be afraid of," she says softly, sweeping my hair behind my ears. "I won't be late. Karen's here to babysit. You like Karen. You can paint some new pictures."

"I don't want to paint any new pictures," I splutter. "I like the old ones."

"I know, the old ones are beautiful," she says. "But

you haven't made me a picture in a whole week. That's not like you."

"I forget how," I say.

"Oh, I can't imagine that you have," she says. "You've just been a little disrupted."

"Why do you have to go?" I plead with her.

"Because there are things I need to do," she explains.

"But why can't you take me with you?" I beg.

"I am taking you with me, Thelma. In here," she says, tapping her chest. "Like I always do, everywhere I go. Can't you do the same thing? Keep me here?" she asks, putting her finger to my chest.

—

Karen is here. She has detached the earphones from her Walkman so we can each listen to Nirvana with one ear. I'm not all that interested. I generally prefer the friendlier sounds of Big Bird. "No—right here, this part, listen to it, oh my God, it's so cool," she gushes.

"Yeah, I guess so," I defer.

"Kurt Cobain, oh my God, he's like immortal," she says with dreamy intensity.

She makes me burnt toast with Marmite for dinner, my favourite. She is doing her homework across the table from me and I am trying to do a very complicated drawing of two hearts floating on top of an ocean full of sharks, when she says, "He's actually kind of cute for an old guy. Well, not *old* old."

"Who?" I ask.

"Your mum's date," she says.

"What's a date?" I ask her.

"Well, like a guy and a girl . . . " she thinks aloud. "Well, like a guy and a girl go out together and, I dunno, see a movie or something and then maybe at the end of it, you know, smooch-a-rama or something."

"Smooch-a-what?"

"Like kissing."

"My mum is kissing?" I ask, horrified.

"I dunno," says Karen. "Maybe. Who knows. People probably have different ideas about dating when you're as old as she is."

"My mum's not old," I say.

"Well, she's not *old* old," Karen agrees, "But she is, like, a parent."

"She's not old. She's the same as me," I say.

"Well, you look a little like her," Karen laughs. "But you're a little kid, Thelma. She's a grown-up."

"Is that why she's kissing?"

"Guess so," shrugs Karen. "I know. It's gross to think about your parents kissing," she says. "Makes me want to puke, actually."

"My mum's teaching her class," I say.

"Oops," says Karen.

"What?"

"Sorry, I thought you knew."

"Knew what?" I ask.

"Well, that she was on a date. What kind of teacher goes out looking all sexy like that?"

"What's sexy?" I ask her.

"Oh God. Maybe you should ask your mother," says Karen. "On second thoughts, don't. She'll think I've been putting ideas into your head."

"What ideas?"

"About the facts of life," says Karen.

"What's that?"

"Don't you go to school yet?" asks Karen, annoyed by my questions at this point.

"Yeah," I tell her. "Senior kindergarten."

"Well, don't they teach you anything there?"

"Yeah. Adding and subtracting and the alphabet and modelling with clay and stuff," I explain.

"Well, your mum's not telling you the facts," Karen advises.

"What facts?" I ask.

"Like this guy, for instance. My mum says your mum and him are an item. You better ask her."

"What's an item?" I ask.

"Oh, forget it," says Karen, exasperated.

—

I am sleeping like an aspirin, round, white and tiny on Mummy Roo's pillow when she comes in later that night. She is crawling into bed and pulling me down from the pillow and in under the covers. I am waking up.

"Don't wake up, angel," she whispers.

"What are the facts, Mummy?"

"What facts?" she sighs, tired.

"Of life."

"What has Karen been telling you?" she asks me.

"That you were kissing and stuff. And that you're an item."

"Well, I don't think Karen really knows the facts," my mother says. "Can I tell you tomorrow, precious? Mummy's very tired right now."

"From kissing?" I ask her.

"No, sweetheart. Tomorrow, OK? Can't we dream a dream now?"

"About what?" I ask.

"You choose."

"About a big bloody monster who is going to suck the sun out of the sky."

"That doesn't sound like a very happy dream, Thelma. How about a compromise. How about a big bright sun that is going to shrivel up all the monsters and turn them into shiny pennies."

"Into raisins."

"OK, sweetheart. Raisins."

—

He is called a boyfriend. Mummy Roo has a boyfriend called Peter and she wants to introduce him to me. I am screaming at him as he stands there at the front door—" Get away from me! I don't want you!" The four-year-old is screaming, "Don't. Don't let him in here. I don't want a Daddy!"

"You motherfucker, you pig shit, you fucking rapist!" screams the twenty-six-year-old.

"Why don't you want a Daddy, Thelma? What are

you afraid of?" Dr. Novak is asking me gently. "Speak to me, Thelma. What did he do to you?"

"This mouth," I stammer. "There is this dream of a mouth—huge and bloody—tearing apart these stitches that bind it closed. It's just pulling these stitches through its own flesh. It is trying to inhale the world, it is sucking with all its might, sucking everything in. It's going to suck me in. It makes such a terrible noise. Like thunder. It is always the image of this mouth."

"Whose mouth?" she asks me. "Whose mouth is it?"

"I don't know. Mine? But I am on the outside of it. It is mine but it's trying to suck me in."

"What happens, Thelma? What gets sucked in?"

"Him," I say in quiet shock.

"Your father?" she asks me.

"Every speck of vile sperm that has ever dropped in this fucking world. It's all here," I say, pointing to my lips. I know them cracked and swollen. I know the feel of these lips. The taste. The salt burning.

Who Needs a U-Haul?

Heroin heard the call of my wild. She is my wild. She is my unspoken one. She is my stoic, silent soldier. She heard me speak and she came home to me to open wide her wild mouth and scream the scream of our lifetime. She came to me in the middle of last night—the last night of the dreaming. It's been years and years since I have seen her open her mouth, and what comes out now seems something more like an unrehearsed growl than speech.

I would celebrate her emergence from silence more if she wasn't so insistent upon using my body as a vehicle through which to express herself. She's not as savvy and sophisticated as I had imagined. She is actually rather crass and given to hysterical outbursts at moments even I consider inappropriate. Corinna suggests that maybe we'd prefer to eat in my room and Heroin spits at her as she stands there with a tray of ravioli and brown bread. "Must you always patronize me!" she yells, and slams the door in Corinna's face.

I feel quite torn. Corinna is only doing her, albeit limited, best. But in my room Heroin says, "Look, it's an impossible situation. I feel quite stifled here."

"They're only trying to be kind," I defend.

"Sure. But food offerings aren't going to erase a history of starvation."

"It's temporary."

"OK. But till when. And to what end? How does this actually help you?"

"I know it's frustrating. But it probably gives me a certain amount of safety and comfort."

"Is it really comforting? To be patronized, treated like a child or someone mentally ill? There is no room here for a life that is any different."

"What do you suggest?"

"You move out. Get a place with me."

"With what resources?"

"Jesus, Thelma, you get a job. You do what other people do. You know—a life?"

"But I'm terrified."

"I know, Thel. I'll help you. I'll go to work with you and be charming and hyperefficient and you can have the rest of the time for not feeling like a grown-up."

—

I am surprised to find Corinna and Warren expressing some kind of relief. Warren says, "Well, this really is a positive step forward," and Corinna seizes the opportunity to consider off-loading her chipped, mismatched plates.

I have a job. I am articling four days a week at a firm downtown and studying during the rest of the week. It's a small practice partnered by four robust women, with whom I came absolutely clean about my troubles. I did what Heroin said: Tell them this is where you come from, this is where you are, this is where you could go. They said straight out: This is what we want from you, this is how we can help you, and this is how we can't help you. It is all a question of sorting out and compartmentalizing. Knowing when and where I can splash in the bath and holler.

November first is moving day. I have told Warren and Corinna that I don't need their help. Heroin still has her horse, after all, and believe me, that stallion could haul a planet. Corinna is packing a big cardboard box with odds and ends. I am grateful to her, although I don't feel any compelling need for a lettuce drier without a lid, a single oven mitt or a rusty cheese grater. I stop her at the small Persian rug, though.

"Mum, you love that rug," I say.

"I want you to have it, Thelma," she says.

"But it's yours. It's . . . you."

"What? You don't want anything of me in your new place?" she says, a little hurt.

"That's not it, Mum. I just want things to be simple at first. And then I'll decide how I want to decorate."

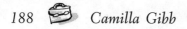

She is pulling away. I want to tap my chest and say "in here," but I know she wouldn't get it. I feel sorry for her then. She is starting to look old to me.

Thelma Takes up Room

Here is my tiny house. A white room with blue linen curtains that I have made myself. A hardwood floor that I have just sanded and revarnished, and black and white linoleum floors in the little closets called the kitchen and the bathroom. There is a tiny postage stamp of a balcony on which I can sit on a wicker chair and look down on Heroin's horse grazing in the back yard while she is away at work being charming and hyperefficient.

When Heroin comes home from work we have a glass of red wine on the balcony and she tells me about her day. She looks different now, and I'm not used to her talking this much. I think she has a bit of a crush on Mary, one of the partners in the practice, because she's mumbling a lot of Mary this and Mary that and staring off into space. "You're not even listening, Thelma!" she yells. But I am lost in my own reverie about a remarkable woman: wondering how I can be growing so much taller. Hoping I can outgrow this man called boyfriend.

"You know, I'm reading this case history," Heroin blathers on, despite my lack of attention. "And I'm saying to Mary, Well, legally she can't really deny access, and she says to me, Just take a minute to see if you can try and imagine how she might feel."

"Yeah," I nod, imagining myself as a poisonous undercooked pork chop served up on a man-sized platter.

"What about you, Thel?" she asks. "What about your day?"

"Painted an excellent picture. Flushed the rest of the drugs."

"That's great, Thelma," she says, pausing. "You know, you really ought to try coming in to work with me." She doesn't want me to miss it. She thinks it will do me a world of good and she is tired of having to be the charming and efficient one all the time. "You can still be a dreamy spacecake on your lunch break," she assures me. "You could even make your collages in the back room, you know."

Every day I am more willing. I am becoming increasingly curious about the world beyond my imagination. There is a code for living, which is constructed strangely, and perhaps there are maps and schedules to guide people through it. People appear to

do it effortlessly; they have cracked the code unknow-
ingly and they act as if the rhythm of living is their
own. I don't know yet where their imaginary friends
live. Not in offices, that's for sure.

I swallow Heroin in order to gain strength. I'm not
going to work in her clothes, though. She's all tweed
suits and sensible shoes. I am much more quirky, a
little out of place in a law office, undoubtedly, but if
I'm going to really do it, I'm going to do it in my own
shoes. Boots, actually, chunky and black, which I wear
with a long black tunic over a starched, white,
oversized shirt and black leggings. I wear big lashes of
black liquid liner and carry a black rubber knapsack.
And I am into hats. I wear an orange, black and gold
cap today and clip my hair back.

"What a great hat," Mary comments, not recognizing
my total image overhaul, as she plops down a stack of
manilla file folders on my desk. "Briefs on all our same-
sex custody cases," she says. "All husbands seeking
custody after their wives have either left them for
women or come out as lesbian after they were
separated or divorced. This one's completely different,
though," she says, referring to her latest case. "This
could be huge." She looks a little too hungry and I find
it disarming.

I am diving head first into the research for this case.
It is the murky and contested terrain of two mothers, a
landscape I traverse with some sense of the familiar.
Lovers who have lost their love for each other but share

the love for the child they have raised together. The child is not the biological child of either woman, but it is legally H's child, since only one woman is officially recognized as a mother in this province. M, however, has been the one who has acted as primary caregiver, giving up her job so she could be at home raising the baby Sadie.

H and M are ferocious. Tearing chunks out of each other in their accusations. Using the secrets shared in some earlier place of trust to malign each other, each condemning the other as a less suitable mother. H is resurrecting painful details about M's psychiatric history, which, unfortunately for our client, is admissible testimony. We have a file bulging with letters in support of M. Her present is watertight, but her past is leaking and threatening to drown who she is today and who she is in relation to this child.

I know about drowning. I am barely floating myself. Every day I take a measurement of the water level and sometimes I have to wear heels just to keep my head above it. I am managing and I am not quite sure how, because I feel like a fraud with two-thirds of my body under water.

I am to record M's version of her psychiatric past. She comes into the office, obviously drained from the events of recent weeks, but nevertheless striking and elegant. She is tall and thin with cropped black hair and grey eyes framed by long, thick lashes. She wears big chunks of silver, a short black skirt and a houndstooth jacket, and her skin is luminescent, her lips and eyelids dusted with silver powder. I am somewhat intimidated but I have the strength and presence of Heroin within me to keep me focused. She looks familiar to me.

I offer her a cup of coffee, which she takes black, and we sit informally, her at one end of the green leather couch and me in the armchair with a pad of paper on my lap. I am listening to her story, about having been bulimic and depressed. It is too familiar to break my heart, told in a language I know too well, so it disturbs me less than it probably should. Heroin has to stifle my natural inclination to confide in her. To splutter out, "Hey, I've been in hospital, too." To tell her about Dr. N. To ask her whether she's ever lived in a cave. Heroin tells me to shut up. Dr. N. is more gentle, reminding me: This is her story. This is not your story. Remember not to collapse yourself into her narrative or appropriate it as your own.

"I just need to get the facts straight first," I say with affected professional calm. "Will you give me the dates and the reasons or diagnoses attached to your hospital-izations?"

"Yes, of course," she says without any apparent discomfort, and begins to speak.

Molly. This is Molly, who wheeled herself and her IV past me and had been an unusual friend to me in a time and a place where I didn't know myself or anyone else. That was Molly, and this confident and calm woman before me is Molly, and the only resemblance is the dead in the grey of her eyes.

"Molly?" I say, looking up from my pad of paper.

"Yes?" she asks, not understanding the reason for the shift in my tone of voice.

"Molly, I'm Thelma. Thelma Barley. From the hospital? 1987?" She looks at me as if she is flipping through a rolodex in her head. "Maybe you wouldn't remember," I offer. "Dr. Walker? Purple vomit?" I prompt.

"Oh my God," she says with some confusion. "But you don't look anything like Thelma Barley."

"Well, no. I wasn't well then. Maybe I wasn't even Thelma Barley then."

"Oh my God," she repeats, attempting to reconcile two dramatically different worlds.

"It's OK," I say, reaching out to squeeze her hands folded in her lap.

"It's just that I was so mean to you that day you were leaving," she says.

"I understand it now," I say, reassuringly. "I really do."

—

"Oh my God, delicious," Molly says, sliding a piece of fish into her mouth. We're having lunch.

"It's so good to see you enjoying food."

"Yeah, well, it took time," she says, casting her eyes downward. "You too, huh?"

I nod. "I had a real problem putting things in my mouth."

"Yeah, I know what that's about."

"I'm sure you do."

Molly covers her mouth for a minute and then smiles. "Recognize me now?" she beams.

"Ugh, Molly. That's awful!" I shudder at the site of her toothless gums, her dentures cupped in her outstretched hand.

"It's pretty gross, isn't it?" she laughs sarcastically.

"It's disgusting!" I can't resist shrieking.

She sticks her teeth back in and says, "Talk to me about mouths. I ruined my fucking teeth. I've been known to pop out my teeth at parties if some man dares suggest I just haven't met the right man." *Go on and kiss me, big boy,* she mouths.

As we leave, she tells me that she is proud of me. "Look at you, Thelma," she says. "You're a lawyer, you look great, you sound great."

"You think so?" I ask, surprised. "Gee, thanks. I'm not actually a lawyer yet, I still have my bar exams to get through at the end of this year. And to be honest, I don't know what the fuck I'm doing most of the time."

"That's OK," she says. "Nobody really does. You'd be surprised."

"Yeah, I guess so."

"If you want it enough . . . " She trails off.

"What is it?"

"It's my baby," she sighs. "You can't imagine how the

thought of losing her breaks my heart. I promised Sadie I would never leave. I promised this child that I would never leave and now I have to fight for my life to keep her."

"What's Harriet's motivation?" I ask her.

"It's complicated. Harriet is very intelligent, very driven, very career-oriented. I admire her ambition, and we've been able to live really well, and I've had the privilege of staying home with Sadie, but for her, having a child is like earning some kind of Girl Guide badge. She doesn't admit this, but I really think having a child, like having a middle-class home and a cottage, represents 'normal' for her and she desperately wants to be normal. She really doesn't want to be a lesbian. She's not out. Her colleagues actually think Sadie is her biological child—she renders me absolutely invisible even though I'm the one doing all the parenting. For all I know she probably tells them Molly is Sadie's daycare supervisor."

"Do you think she's jealous of your relationship with Sadie?" I ask her.

"Oh, there's no question that she's jealous. She's jealous of the relationship, but she's not jealous of the work involved in developing and sustaining that relationship."

"So how would you characterize her as a mother?" I ask, slipping out my notepad.

"Distant, preoccupied. Unstable."

"Unstable is precisely the word she is levelling against you."

"Harriet has had a string of lovers since our breakup."

"And you?" I ask, although I am little embarrassed at having to.

"Me? No. God. I've been far too concerned with this whole thing," she says.

"And Harriet isn't concerned?"

"She's concerned about one thing. Being adored. Publicly, privately. She doesn't want this to escalate because it could be publicized, but if she doesn't fight it, how is she suddenly going to explain the fact that she only sees her daughter on alternate weekends now."

"So either way she risks being outed."

"Yeah, and you know I understand it. I have always respected her wish for privacy, but it sickens me that she is using Sadie to protect herself," Molly says, shaking her head.

I have known a mother to give her child away, surrender her in the extreme, cook the meal for which her daughter is destined to be dessert. In order to save herself, her face, her version of the world, Corinna colluded in submitting to the swollen penis of the Devil. Molly is another mother, less bound, and more willing to fight. "How far are you prepared to take this?" I ask her.

"Whatever the distance," she's says with determination.

"But you know all this stuff about your psychological history will get dredged up and picked apart in court. Once you have mental illness stamped on your forehead, virtually everything you do will be seen in court as pathologically motivated somehow."

"Don't I know it. If it wasn't for the fact that I was really able to make something of myself as a journalist, I wouldn't be very far away from seeing myself as mentally ill. And being a mother is hardly seen as a credible identity."

"God," we say simultaneously.

—

Heroin is waiting for me at home, stretched out on the couch wearing my 501s with a glass of cranberry juice balanced on her stomach. "Hey, style queen! You look like you've had a good day," she says.

I just beam.

"What did I tell you?" she teases.

"Move over," I nudge her. I lie there beside her watching the white sheet over my balcony door flutter in the cool early evening wind. My legs are wrapped around Heroin's legs for warmth and she wakes me some time later and says, "Hey, you're taking up most of the room." I mumble but I do not move.

She can always change shape, but I cannot.

—

I have invited Molly over for dinner. It's Saturday

morning and I wake early, excited by the promise of the day. I want to make pasta and Heroin suggests we go to St. Lawrence market and get some fresh pasta, basil and garlic, and she'll show me how to make really good pesto.

This is new for me. Normally I spend Saturdays in bed with a book, daydreaming about Mummy Roo and writing to her in my journal.

"Oh God, but what will I wear?" I hesitate.

"I hardly think I'm the one to consult for fashion advice," Heroin laughs. "It's a market. It's Saturday. I dunno."

I pull on my jeans and my boots, and a hooded Gap sweatshirt.

"Perfect," Heroin says.

"Wait," I say, and pull on my rose-coloured knit cap. "OK, I'm ready. Andiamo."

I wear black gloves and coast down Spadina Avenue on my bike through the bracing air and then pedal as hard as I can along Front Street against the wind.

The market is thick with warm light, people and colour. I move among and with them. I pick out a large bundle of basil and hand it to the guy behind the cash register. "I love your hat," he says.

"Gee, thanks," I mumble, a little embarrassed.

"The colour's great with your eyes," he says, handing me the change.

"Thanks a lot," I say, shyly, and wander off. "Was he flirting with me?" I ask Heroin.

"Duh. Obviously. Have a look at him."

I turn around and he is looking at me. He smiles. I smile back and then laugh, embarrassed.

———

I want it to be perfect. I have never invited someone over for dinner. So I buy flowers and Spanish Rioja and clear off my desk and cover it with a white sheet. I play my favourite Leonard Cohen CD and sing out loud. I feel happy. This might be the happiest day I have ever had. Probably a mistake to call Corinna just then, but I haven't called her in two weeks.

"How's it going, Mum?" I ask her.

"Oh," she says, sounding annoyed. "So you finally found a moment in your schedule to return my call."

"Sorry. It's just been really intense at work."

"How is it that you're so self-important all of a sudden?"

"I'm into my job, that's all," I defend.

"Well, Thelma, you know what happened last time you worked too hard. You almost tore your eyes out."

"Do you have to bring that up again? How many years ago was that? I like what I'm doing."

"Well, I don't like the sound of it. All these self-important women. How do you expect to get any respect as a lawyer if you work with a bunch of lesbians."

"They're not a bunch of lesbians, Mum. They're feminists. There's a fucking difference," I say angrily.

"Well, it must be a pretty fine distinction."

"Mum, they're feminists, you know, like they don't go for things like boob jobs!" I shout, immediately regretting it.

"You're just jealous because men don't look at you!"

"Mum—I have to go now," I say, doing my utmost to restrain myself.

"Oh yes, so busy and self-important now. Getting ready for a big date, are you?"

"I do have a date, as a matter of fact," I say. Just not the kind of date she imagines, where a guy picks me up in his car and I wear a miniskirt and heels and I listen to him talk about himself all night and then he pulls out his Visa and then his penis shortly thereafter and I feel like I can't protest the latter because I haven't protested the former. I have a date where a friend from my past comes for dinner and we drink wine and lie on the floor, hold each other's hand and talk for hours. I have a friend. I have a friend.

———

"I don't care if they call me crazy," Molly says. "All the people who I've ever felt were worth knowing have been called crazy at some point in their lives. Nobody knows what the fuck they're doing. We can only hope that there's a masterpiece somewhere in the mess we always make."

And when we are nearly through the second bottle of wine she starts to cry. "You know, I'm beginning to think that I was right all along. People don't stay," she says sadly. "But maybe not because they don't care, but because sometimes they don't have a choice. Look how hard I'm trying to hold on to my little girl and look how determined Harriet is to ensure Sadie feels I've abandoned her."

"Something must stay," I say, earnestly looking into her eyes. "Whatever happens, Sadie can keep you here," I say, reaching out. "It's the only way we can hold on to each other. I dunno. Therapy," I shrug, a little embarrassed. Molly reaches out to hug me and I put my arms around her awkwardly. Not a familiar feeling, but not altogether unpleasant.

"You're such a fucking therapy head," she laughs.

Fish Girls

People get ugly in love. Molly issues subtle threats and Harriet starts to yield. Molly doesn't feel proud of herself for doing it, but she will not sit quietly and let her life and Sadie's be determined by Harriet's fear.

Mary is a little disappointed that the case won't be the big Supreme Court challenge that she had envisioned. I am arguing with her about this: Is it worth dragging people's lives through the mud in order to challenge legislation? Aren't we just exploiting them? She cannot believe that I would even ask this. "It's a constitutional challenge!" she shouts. "It's a human rights issue—how can we ever expect to effect attitudinal change if we don't fight for legal recognition?"

"Still, we're talking about sacrificing individual lives in order to do it," I defend.

"Thelma, you've lost sight of the point of this case.

Don't get too attached to the personalities involved," she says.

"We're friends," I tell her. "I mean, we met years ago and we're becoming good friends."

"The best thing you can do for her as a friend, Thelma, is not lose sight of the broader implications of this case."

I have to be careful.

—

We take Sadie to Toronto Island the following Saturday. She's throwing bits of her chocolate-glazed doughnut at the ducks. "I don't know if they really like chocolate, sweetheart," Molly says to her.

"He's eating it!" Sadie shrieks with delight.

"So he is," says Molly. "God, I'm so pathetic. I don't want her to feel rejected by ducks," she says to me.

"She really is your daughter," I say as Sadie throws her arms round Molly's legs, squishing her chocolate-covered mouth into Molly's white pants. Molly takes my hand and I squeeze it.

She drops me off later at home and I cannot help saying to her, "I wish I didn't have to leave you both."

"I know," she says. "You're being a great support to me, Thelma. Especially when I feel like I can't be much of a friend to anyone right now."

—

Sadie makes me a little nervous. I don't know why exactly. She's wide-eyed and trusting and she calls me

"Telly, Telly, Telly" whenever she sees me, and says, "Pick me up. Give me an airplane."

I'm not altogether easy with this. I swing her round by the arms and hold up her legs when she does a headstand, but I don't know what to do when we meet eye to eye with her face very close to mine. She is easy and affectionate and rubs her nose against mine. It makes me laugh, embarrassed. Something about it feels slightly wrong. Slightly perverse, or illicit somehow. But she asks for it, she demands it, she shouts, "Hug!" "Kiss!" at least once every ten minutes. She wraps herself around Molly's leg and says, "Walk, Mummy," and clings like a barnacle as Molly limps around the kitchen saying, "Oh my God, you are such a heavy potato." She is a potato, she is a sweet sweet little potato latke.

She wants to build a snowman but we settle for a snow bunny because there is barely an inch of snow. Carrots for ears. "And he lives in the cabbage patch with all his cabbagey friends," she natters. "And in the summer he lives in our fridge. Next to the eggs. And he eats all the cheese and Mummy says, Oh no, where's all the cheese gone? No grilled cheese for dinner."

"So what's for dinner then?" I ask her.

"Maybe just acorns and some chazelnuts," she says.

"Hmm. I think the squirrels might have buried them all," I comment.

"Oh silly. Not squirrel nuts, Bloblaws nuts. In big bags."

Sadie loves Loblaws. In fact, I've started to like it too, shopping for food on Saturday mornings with Molly. Squashing Sadie's chubby little thighs through the seat holes in the shopping cart. Molly at one end of the aisle and me at the other, Sadie squealing with delight as the cart flies back and forth between us.

Sadie has swimming lessons at the university pool on Saturday mornings and I have taken to going with her and Molly before we go shopping. Molly goes into the water sometimes—it's a mothers and toddlers thing.

"Thel? Would you mind going in today?" Molly asks me one morning. "I feel like crap. I think I've OD'd on echinacea."

"Uh, well, I don't really swim," I say, apologetically.

"You don't?" she asks, surprised.

"Well, I do, but not usually in water. Maybe once or twice."

Swimming scares me. It reminds me of dismembered floating body parts, it reminds me of blood in my head. I am afraid that the water will rush in and fill up my nose and mouth, I am afraid to take off my clothes. The smell of chlorine is familiar and sickening. I cannot tell her this. If I swallow any water, I will vomit. If I taste chlorine, I will die.

"Well, why don't you try? You're in the shallow end. You don't actually have to take your feet off the floor, or put your head under or anything."

"You mean I can just stand there?" I ask her.

"Yup. And she'll swim to you."

Sadie looks like she has more than four limbs going. There is an awful lot of squealing and splashing. I'm wearing Molly's blue polka-dot bathing suit, standing up to my waist in water, and Sadie is making her way toward me with her neck stretched and her face looking pained. I am supposed to be encouraging like the other mothers, but all I can manage to say is, "Oh God, Sadie. Please don't drown." I stretch out my arms and grab her hands and she comes rushing toward me, laughing.

"Hey, you're pretty good," I tell her.

"Not so good at floating," she says, out of breath.

"Why don't you pretend you're a twig," I suggest. "A floating twig. Or maybe a dead body."

Oops.

Sadie looks at me, confused. "Maybe a fish," she nods, and starts to swim away from me.

Hmm. A fish girl can move. A fish girl can swim away.

I am supposed to hold her under the stomach while she sticks her face in the water and blows bubbles. She coughs and water runs out her nose. I ask her if she's going to throw up. She splutters "No" and coughs some more. Her instructor makes her way over and taps Sadie lightly on the back until she finishes coughing.

"That's why you blow bubbles, Sadie. So the water doesn't get in your nose and your mouth. Isn't that right?" she says, smiling carefully at me.

"I guess so," I say, a little dumbly.

—

So the water doesn't get in your nose and your mouth.
Hmm. So you are not poisoned. So you don't drown.
You float: Animated, alive and slippery. You tear
through shark-infested waters and know where to find
solitude and respite in cool green pools with names like
the Crying Pond and the Lonely Lagoon. You swim
through the legs of wicked men wearing rubber boots
and break the surface to blow cyanide bubbles in their
faces. They choke on your poisonous breath and
collapse face first into their own troubled waters. They
are dead men whose fat corpses rot slowly, their chins
receding one by one, a thick oily film, their legacy of
ten thousand English breakfasts of bacon and fried
bread on the surface of the water. No one comes to
rescue them. The terrified child still lies in bed awake
at night, afraid to fall asleep. Sometimes the child's
heartbeat returns, but never for long, because she can
never be sure that Daddy isn't coming home. Her
heartbeat will never be regular. She will dream of
bodies, alive and rotting.

People don't understand dead. They think it is all or
nothing. I used to move between live and dead several
times in the course of a day. Sometimes the transition
was as brief and unremarkable as a sigh or a sentence.
I must not speak to Sadie of the dead. I must pretend
that, like her, I know nothing of their existence. I must
do laps of living beside her.

—

It's not a total victory but it is a total celebration. It is April, and Molly has invited us all to her house to celebrate. I am bringing Molly the brightest bunch of yellow and orange flowers I can find and I have stuck some of the marigolds into the purple straw hat I have woven for the occasion. I am wearing a lime-green vintage polyester dress with sequins over the bust. Heroin says to me, "You're not really going out like that, are you?"

"Yeah, why not? You don't like?"

"It kind of teeters on that fine line between eccentric and deranged," she says.

"It's my look," I defend. "Dr. N. says it shows real personality."

"That it certainly does," she says.

—

Molly greets us with outstretched arms: me and Mary and the three other women at the practice. Several of Molly's friends are already there, sipping martinis on the patio in the back yard. The house is filled with music and Molly is radiant. She and Harriet have agreed to equal time with Sadie, and Harriet has given Molly the money for a down payment on this house. She has started freelancing and has converted the attic into a bright, open work space. She looks happier than I have ever seen her.

"Thelma, I love your hat!" she exclaims as we step out of our embrace. "You've always had such a sense of style," she flatters me.

"Have I really?" I say, blushing.

Mary says, "Well, how do you think you got the job? Not just your brains, my dear. The moment we saw you show up in that red and green jester hat, we thought, This one's either crazy or a keeper." We all laugh. Heroin's obviously been borrowing my clothes.

Molly leads us through a kitchen bustling with activity and out into the back yard. "Everybody," she says to the small crowd gathered there, "meet the women who supported me through this case." She introduces each of us in turn. "But I particularly want to thank Mary and Thelma, who were most directly involved. I wouldn't have had the faith to continue without them," she says, beaming at us. Molly's friends and family start to clap and I am so embarrassed that I can only look at my shoes and wonder if the ground is about to open up and suck me in whole.

"Martinis?" Molly asks us.

"Great," I say.

"Good. Come help me, Thelma?" she asks, and I follow her into the kitchen. She pulls me aside and takes my hands in hers. "You know, you're the one I owe the greatest thanks to, Thelma," she says.

I blush and say, "But you know, everybody's worked just as hard on your behalf."

"The best thing to come out of this whole nightmare is this connection with you. I don't know what I would have done these last few months without you." She reaches out to hug me and says, "I love you, goofy girl," as she squeezes me.

Her brother Philip has made martinis for us and tells me how very glad he is to meet me. How much Molly has told him about me. I am nervous and giddy from all the excitement and attention and by the time I carry the tray out to my colleagues, I have demolished two martinis.

Mary is talking to a tall, thin man who is grilling tandoori chicken on the barbecue. "Madame?" I say, approaching her with the tray. "May I offer you a martini? Olive or a twist?"

"Thank you, Thelma." She introduces me to Molly's other brother, Scott, and I trip over my words as I shake his hand. He has exactly those eyes, Molly's eyes, cool grey pools like a dew-covered English morning meadow.

Mary turns me aside and grips my forearm and whispers, "What is it between you and Molly?"

"What do you mean?" I ask, slightly defensively. What is between us? A love, a grown-up thing, a place for being.

Molly comes up behind us then and says, "Not already discussing your next case, are you?"

Mary laughs and says, "Just conspiring to find a way to secure Thelma a permanent place with us."

"Wow, Thelma. That's fantastic."

"Seriously?" I ask Mary.

"You just ace those exams next month and then we'll see what we can offer you."

"Oh my God, Mary. Thank you."

Oh my God, I am definitely going to fail. I don't know what the fuck I'm doing. Mary has no idea. When I get really intimidated or overwhelmed these days, I just turn into a fish and swim off in the other direction, leaving Thelma's body behind. At least I no longer turn into a corpse. At least if someone sneezes I don't crack and crumble into dust.

"This woman has been like a rock for me," Molly says, her arm around my shoulder as she introduces me to her mother.

I am a rock? I am a rock. I am a solid stone hard lump propping open somebody's porch door or held in the hand of a child who has no other weapon. I am not a rock in a desert, I am a rock in a cave of the world, and there are voices everywhere bouncing off walls and lifting me into action.

—

I wake up later that night with Heroin's muffled voice pleading, 'Thel—Thel, could you budge a little? You're squashing me." She wriggles out from under me.

"Jesus, Thelma, you've got to learn to hold your liquor," she grumbles.

"What happened?" I ask her.

"Well, you just came home and passed out on top of me!"

"But what happened before that?"

"Oh honey, four martinis in quick succession does not suit you. Not a really class act, my dear."

"Well, what do I know?" I defend. "I've never had a martini before." I pause. "Did I completely humiliate myself?"

"No. Molly saw you looking woozy and you said a very loud and gregarious goodbye to everybody. Don't worry, they all thought you were lovely and commented on your charming and unusual fashion sense. And then Molly bid you adieu with a loving kiss on the forehead and stuck you in a taxi."

Kissed a princess goodnight and willed her to sleep through a ride across a city night where she tumbled into bed and slept on a pea.

"God, I hope I didn't embarrass her," I wince.

Not Designed for Comfort

I am telling Dr. N. about family as if I am the first to discover it. I have seen family and friends celebrating together. I have felt their warmth and generosity. Watched it rise like irrepressible bubbles surging upward from a hot spring. "My family is incredible," Molly had said.

"I want family. I want this feeling," I tell Dr. N. She is happy for me. "I want a big house where you and I live with Molly and Sadie and we have lots of animals. Roger the tortoise and Teddy the boy-cat and a parakeet named Cocker Spaniel. And Heroin."

"A house full of women?" Dr. N. asks me.

"Yeah."

"You lived in a house full of women once," she reminds me. "The vicarage."

"No. We weren't women. We were ghosts." I don't remember women. I remember white dust swirling by me on the staircase. Particles of cremated bodies getting caught in my hair. I remember noises coming out of walls, not out of people's mouths. I remember feeling blind in a maze of unintelligible languages. Our trade—voodoo dolls.

"I thought Jesus was watching," I reflected. Watching me like a stalker, waiting for the glimpse of my nakedness that would make him rise.

"But you don't have religious beliefs, do you, Thelma?" she asks, although she knows perfectly well that I don't.

"No," I say. "He was just a guy who didn't know when enough was enough."

"So he was just a guy."

"Yeah."

"And just being a guy is creepy?"

"Sometimes. I mean, I don't think Jesus would freak me out now, but I still wouldn't feel like asking him over to dinner."

"Is there anyone you would ask over for dinner?"

"Maybe Patrick."

"Have you heard from him lately?"

"He calls sometimes. He doesn't sound very happy, though."

"Has he ever?"

That I don't know, actually. Too much noise in my head to ever hear him. "Fuck, poor Patrick," I say, sadly. "I mean, he hardly knew what he was up against. There were just a whole lot of us talking at the same time and cancelling each other out. Oh God. You know, I used to see other men living in his eyes. I mean literally, there'd be little heads in his irises with nasty smirks on their faces. I didn't blame him. He didn't know they were there. I just thought he'd been like, invaded by fucking body snatchers."

"Do you think you might have put the men in his eyes?"

"No. I mean, I was obviously the only one who saw them there. But I didn't put them there. There's no way I could have put them there."

Or could I? I had to peer deep, beyond my superficial reflection, in order to see them. They were lurking insidiously in the places I wanted to look. Staring back at me with lascivious grins and running their tongues over my reflection and around the rims of Patrick's eyes.

—

I want to swim the ocean now. I want to scale the cliffs of Dover and ride Heroin's horse over fields of damp green grass to the towers in the distance. I want Patrick to open the tower door to me and I want to see clarity in his eyes. I want his eyes to be a mirror. I want to make sure his body has not been invaded by others. I want to make sure his insides have not been ravaged by the men I might have put there.

"Are you happy, Patrick?" I ask him on the phone.

"What a strange question," he laughs.

"Strange?"

"Well, yes, coming from you," he says, though not meanly.

"I'm just concerned," I say. "I want to know that you're happy."

"Well, I wouldn't concern yourself with that, Thelma. I don't know that I ever expect to be happy. I thought you didn't either."

"No, I don't suppose I do," I reflect. "But there are moments."

"You're funny," he says.

"I miss you," I tell him.

"Yeah, I miss you too, baby."

—

Molly asks me if I'm serious. "I have to see him again," I tell her. "I just have to know that he's all right."

"Are you sure you can handle it all, though? You have a lot of negative associations with that place."

It does make me feel sick to think of England. But I like the thought of Molly coming with me. I want her to meet Patrick. I want to make a sandwich out of the people I love, with me as the squishy filling soaking this blessed bread.

"Of course I'll come with you, Thelma. But you know, just make sure it's what you want to do."

Heroin won't be coming. She's far too exhausted. She says she must have made that trip about fifteen hundred times by now. She's three feet tall now and looks adorable and I make her a cup of hot chocolate but she acts like it is too heavy for her to lift.

"He'll miss not seeing you," I tell her, still trying to convince her.

"Honey, he was barely aware of my presence," she tells me. "I'm afraid you stole my thunder."

I stole Heroin's thunder. I stole the power of stomping hooves travelling at light speed over the cavernous fields, trampling all obstacles on the path.

"It's OK. You can take my horse," she offers.

—

"Bless you for coming with me," I say, squeezing Molly's hand.

"Just get me another vodka," she says. "I can't stand flying." We are flying again, space-time travel, losing hours over miles. After half a Valium and her third vodka, Molly is sleeping against my shoulder and I am afraid to move, afraid I'll wake her. She snores in a rather embarrassing way and when people look over to see who's making the noise, I smile, as if to say, It's not me.

We are spending a day in London before going to Oxford. Molly has never been to London and she wants to "do" the museums and Harrods. We see a Leather Fashion and Fetish exhibit at the Victoria and Albert and I am shocked. Not the land of double cream and scones and grey sunless faces that I know. Not the public-school-cum-biscuit, headmaster-who-fondles, repressed world of British sex which simultaneously creates, titillates and destroys an empire. This is brazen, this is female, this is—when Molly forces me to look—even a little bit exciting.

Inspired, Molly drags me to the lingerie department at Harrods. I can't seem to justify spending fifty-six pounds on a pair of underwear but Molly insists that it will make me feel sexy. I feel a little bit ridiculous. "The best thing is, no one has to know," she says, as she parades in front of the mirror in a leopard skin bra. I can't look.

We drink beer and remind each other that we are on holiday in order to justify sharing a plate of chips. This feels really criminal. We are seated in a booth at the Ox and Hammer and it is standing room only as men in suits crowd in for lunch. "This is so civilized," says Molly. "These people know how to live."

A large man with curly black hair, greying at the front, nudges his friend and points to our booth. "Do you mind if we join you, ladies?" his friend asks us.

Just as I'm about to say, *We were just leaving*, Molly says, "Of course, gentlemen. And we wouldn't say no to another drink either, would we, Thelma?"

"Right. Bitter, then?" the large man asks.

"Lovely," Molly says, smiling, as he and his friend make their way to the bar.

"Molly! What are you doing! Why are you encouraging them?" I exclaim, although they are barely out of earshot.

"Encouraging what?" she defends. "It's a drink.

They're sharing our table. I'm just having fun. Getting to know the locals."

"You can't do that." I shake my head at her.

"Why not?" she demands.

"Well, they could be rapists or something."

"Oh, Thelma. They are probably two boring advertising executives who come here every day for lunch and consume a thousand calories before going back to their desks to fart their way through the afternoon. Trust me, we have just made their day."

They return to the table carrying four pints and introduce themselves as Peter and Paul.

"I know, it's pretty bloody funny," Peter, the large man, says. "I won't be offended if you make a joke." They sit down beside us and Peter says, "So are you ladies American, then?"

"Canadian," I say.

"Oh, sorry," he says. "I know that's terribly offensive. On holiday?"

"It's sort of a reconnaissance mission," says Molly.

"Well, I lived here for a couple of years," I explain. "I was a student at Oxford."

"Paul was at Cambridge. Got a first in Iranian Studies."

Paul blushes and says, "Which somehow qualifies one to work in a bank. There's a whole floor of us from Cambridge."

"Did you row?" I ask politely.

"Me? Naah. Too many early mornings for me. Too desperately competitive. I much preferred the library."

Good to be housed between books, I think. Good to be silent among words.

"And what did you read?" he asks me.

"Law," I reply.

"And that allows you to practice in Canada?" Peter asks.

"Well, yeah, same law. Different exams."

"And are you a lawyer, too?" he asks Molly.

"A journalist," she says.

"The really bright sparks at Cambridge all become journalists," says Paul. "Mediocre types like me end up in merchant banking."

———

"What a couple of bores," Molly says, as soon as we get outdoors.

"Oh, I thought they were nice," I say, surprised. "You know, decent."

"You're funny, Thelma," she laughs.

"What?" I ask defensively.

"Well, so much for a couple of rapists. Except maybe they're stalking us now. Maybe what they really wanted to do was throw us on the table and lift up our skirts and have themselves a little poke for lunch."

"Molly, that's not funny! OK! You've made your point." She looks a little smug and I cannot get the image out of my mind.

We walk in silence along the street. Molly links her

arm through mine after a while and says, "Only teasing."

"Don't give me that doe-eyed look," I scoff. "I feel like hitting you."

"Go on, big girl," she prods. "Give me your butch best," she says, jumping in front of me.

"Don't, Molly. You know I could."

"Oh, I know you've got it in you, darling. I'm ready for it," she jokes, holding up her fists.

"I'm not a butch," I sulk.

"OK, you're a femme with a mean temper," she says.

"When have you ever seen me with a temper?"

"Come on."

"Come on what?"

"Hit me, call me a name or something, tell me to fuck off," she says, hopping from one foot to the other.

"But I don't want to."

"Well, you did a minute ago."

"The moment passed."

"Practice for next time. So you'll be ready."

"Molly, stop it!" I shout. "This is getting annoying."

"Right on, Thelma. What else?"

"Sometimes you're just such a . . . a lesbian," I say weakly.

"Ooh, now that's fighting talk," she coos.

"I didn't mean to say that. I mean, you're . . . just so aggressive sometimes," I explain.

"I'm just street smart, Thelma. It's just a question of knowing who your enemies are. I'll show you street smart," she says. "Come on, take my arm." She takes a big step and says, "When you step on a crack, you break your mother's back. When you step on a line—"

"I know, you break your father's spine." I reply. "Just a stupid kid's rhyme."

"But it's powerful. I've killed a lot of people this way. I've killed my Uncle Harold at least a thousand times. It's therapy, Thelma. And better that than a life sentence."

"Do you teach Sadie this?" I ask her.

"No, darling. Only kids like you and me. And do you remember this one?" She picks up the pace. "We don't stop for boy-eez," she sings.

"And we don't stop for nobody," I refrain.

"Yeah, well we don't stop for rapists and child molesters and Uncle Harry," she says.

"Yuck," I scowl.

Later, over dinner, I ask her, "Is that why you're a lesbian?"

"Because of Uncle Harry?"

"I guess."

"No. Uncle Harry is certainly part of who I am but he's not the reason I fancy the pants off women."

"Ugh, Molly. You're so crude," I say. "Please don't say anything like that in front of Patrick. He's ... sensitive."

"I don't really care *why* I'm a lesbian, Thelma," she says, ignoring my comment. "If you think people are gay because they were sexually abused, then you should be a prime candidate."

I remember once telling Corinna that I wanted to be a lesbian when I grew up. What I wanted was to curl up like a cat on her lap, and nuzzle my face in the warmth of her armpit. That was all I wanted, but I had no words for it. I'm not sure I want anything more than that. I liked the feel of Patrick's strong arm around me in a protective embrace. I liked the curious feeling in my stomach of inhaling the unfamiliar scent of a man's skin.

Patrick. Tomorrow is Patrick. I am awake in the middle of the night feeling sick but instead of throwing up I decide to wash my hair. Four times. I don't know what to do with myself. I cannot sit still. On the bus to Oxford I make it my project to pick threads out of the fabric of the seat back in front of me. We have just passed the Warneford Hospital and are coasting down Headington Hill into the city centre. I remember the buffed aluminum, the frozen peas and screams that made my hair stand on end. I feel sick with the memory of a world not quite far enough away, but far enough, to be another world.

"It's the next stop," I tell Molly.

"You OK?" she asks me.

"I'm fine. Just be there with me, OK?"

"Right beside you."

Patrick opens the door and beams, "Thelma. Thelma of Distinction."

The house is soft blues and greens and sunlight is streaming through the windows of the sitting room. I remember these colours but not the sunlight. Patrick makes coffee. Molly takes a sip when he is out of the room and pulls a face.

"Instant," I explain. "I have no idea why. They are just obsessed with Nescafé."

"Tastes like crap," she says. "But he's gorgeous."

Yes. Long and lean and chiselled in the doorway. I see him looking at me lovingly and saying, "It's so good to see you, Thelma."

We drive to the White Horse in Abingdon for lunch. It is my favourite pub and although it is November, we sit outside. Patrick asks Molly about Sadie and Molly becomes very animated, telling Sadie stories.

"Patrick, she's just this incredibly brave feisty little grown-up person," I add.

"Thelma!" he says, surprised. "You were terrified of my sister's kids."

"I know," I say apologetically.

"Well, I wouldn't worry. They *are* mutants," he laughs. "Philip is now obsessed with dog poo and Suzanne insists on frilly dresses."

"Too bad it isn't the reverse!" jokes Molly.

We take a drive through Oxford in the afternoon. It really is quite glorious. I am encouraged by Molly's reaction as she catches sight of building after building. She makes me look up. I never used to. I saw only pavement before, grey pavement and people's tired feet trundling home with Tesco's bags full of pathetic overpriced vegetables in their arms. I used to imagine them boiling everything into tasteless mush and eating in sad silence in front of an electric heater.

Patrick and I try to outdo each other playing Oxford geography. Somerville and Indira Gandhi, Magdalen and Oscar Wilde, but the most compelling association of all is Lewis Carroll and Port Meadow. I remember sitting on the Walton Well Road bridge leading to the meadow, knowing it was a bridge not high enough. A different geography. "This is the bridge Clare the howler chucked herself off," I point out to Molly.

"Oh, God. How awful," Molly flinches. "But what *was* she thinking? It's only about sixteen feet," she marvels.

"You know, you can spend every waking hour thinking about killing yourself and still get your calculations wrong. Maybe we actually want to miscalculate," I say aloud. "And why here? Look at the beauty of this meadow. It's just haunting. In the morning a narrow band of mist hangs above it. Chops everybody off at the shoulders and puts their heads in the clouds. In the spring it's covered in blue thistles. And the horses run wild here." I remember lying here, ear to the ground, listening to Heroin gallop, the earth trembling with her intent.

"We can walk by the canal," Patrick suggests. "See the barges."

The canal is in the middle of a jungle of wet

vine-covered trees. "You mean people live here all year round?" Molly asks, incredulous.

"Yeah. I know. I used to wonder how people could walk across the meadow in total darkness and find their way home. I knew of women who lived out here on their own."

There are mailboxes on the bank, and cultivated gardens, and cats and dogs with owners who inscribe bowls with their affectionate names.

"Otherworldly," Molly comments. "I thought *I* was courageous."

It is courageous to make a different world. To make a home across a dark meadow. To live alone along the lonely banks of a canal and make your way home through bracken and wild things.

We walk past the first row of barges and take a path that cuts away from the canal. "Oh my God!" shrieks Molly. "An oasis! What a country!" she exclaims at the site of a pub. "I can't resist," she says.

"All roads lead to a pub. Even in a meadow," Patrick says.

I laugh. Patrick puts his arm around me and pulls me into his shoulder. I close my eyes for a second and inhale the damp.

It is late afternoon and we drink whiskey by the fireplace, damp soles warming in the heat. It grows darker, wetter and more English outside.

"Goofball," says Molly. "Who would give this up?"

"I know," I sigh. "It didn't quite look like this when I was last here. It can feel really oppressive."

"It can," agrees Patrick. Heavy skies narrow the distance to the ground. People shrink under the weight of clouds filled with lies and secrets.

We are all a little drunk. Molly links arms with us both and asks Patrick to teach us football chants as we make our way back across Port Meadow. We shout, "We are the Man U—haters!" over and over again into the walls of darkness.

"Thissaunbelievable place yuhknow?" Molly slurs when we get home.

"What, Molly?" I ask, laughing.

"Uuhdunknow. Cuhyuse a slizapizza."

"You hungry?"

"Ohfuggit. Juss goddabed," she mumbles, before crashing down on the sofa.

"I'll get her a blanket," says Patrick. He comes back and tucks her in under a duvet.

"She's my best friend," I whisper. "Sorry she's a little sloshed."

"She's charming," Patrick says. "Sit in the kitchen?"

I make tea. I know where the teapot is. It's in exactly the same place, and this fact makes me cry.

"It's OK," says Patrick. "It's just a teapot."

"I know, but I gave you this teapot. I bought it at the Gloucester Green market from that blind guy who does pottery."

"Oh, Thelma," he sighs, pulling me into his arms.

His hard chest. His breastbone. His ribs. I am sure my forehead isn't meant to rest against anything else. "I miss you," I whimper.

"I miss you, too," he whispers.

"Do you still love me?" I ask him.

"Of course. I never stopped."

"Will you take me back then?" I ask, looking up at his clear eyes.

"Oh, baby," he sighs. "How do you know that's what you want?"

"I just know," I say.

"But you're still just figuring out what you want," he says.

"Yeah, but I know."

I am looking at him with open pleading. Asking him to destroy the dam that prevents the stream of me from running into a wide, flowing river.

"I don't think I can," he says slowly, shaking his head.

"You can't?" I ask him, straightening up, pulling away to look at his face.

"I don't think I can go through it again, Thelma. I mean the uncertainty. I don't think I could ever handle your looking at me with loathing again. I don't want to be anyone's devil, not even for a second."

Oh God. I get what I deserve. I have polluted, I am polluting. I have killed, I have destroyed. I deserve this for inflicting pain. I know why Molly steps on cracks. She is saving people. She is saving lives. I, on the other hand, am a murderer, and this is the delivery of my life sentence. I am wailing and Patrick is trying to comfort me but my heart is rushing from my chest into my head and beating against my skull. Beating: Let me out.

"Please Patrick," I beg him. "I will be so good. I will do anything you want me to do."

"No, Thelma," he says, shaking his head. "Don't say that. I don't need you to be good. I don't need you to do anything for me. It makes me really uncomfortable when you say that. I just want you to be Thelma."

"But I can't be Thelma without you," I plead.

"You are. You have to be, Thelma. Whether we're together or not," he says.

"But I can learn to make love," I plead.

"That has nothing to do with it, Thelma. You know."

"But if I could, then maybe you would know that I was committed to you."

"I can know that you are committed as much as you are able, without making love."

"Don't you want to make love to me anymore?" I ask.

"Yes. I do. But I can't."

"Are you afraid of me?"

"I'm not afraid of you. But I can't be with you. I told you why."

"But can't we just make love tonight and maybe you'll change your mind?"

"It would only complicate things. If you ever looked at me again with fear in your eyes, I wouldn't be able to live with myself." He went on. "Thelma, I know you won't be able to understand this, I know you won't understand that I still love you, but I've started seeing someone else."

Oh.

Pardon?

What?

Is that what this is about?

Really?

Who?

When?

How could you?

"Oh my God, I deserve this," I bleat.

"You don't deserve this. It's just timing. And it's not the reason. I told you the reason. Don't think it is because of someone else," he pleads with me.

"But I thought you still loved me," I wail.

"I do. Absolutely. My feelings about you haven't changed."

I think I could cry for the rest of my life. Or at least the next thirty-six hours. Wailing for hours is new for me. Before I would just leave the planet, and emotions are fewer and duller somehow in outer space. I feel like I am going to die. Is this what being alive feels like? Feeling like you are going to die? I blubber my way upstairs with Patrick's arm around me all the way into his bed. I cry at the sight of the bedroom, I cry at the sight of the futon, I cry at the sight of the window, the clock radio, and his socks on the floor. I cry against his hard chest until I can cry no more. And then finally I stop. "Fuck," I say. "I don't mean to be so melodramatic."

"Do you feel better?" he asks me.

"I feel completely wiped out," I say. "This futon is lumpy."

Sleep. Dream of heads that get stretched away from bodies and have conversations with each other in clouds. Long long necks and we are all bald. We all have dark eyebrows. We are all about thirty-something years old.

"Are you in love?" I ask Patrick, after staring at the back of his head for half an hour.

"Oh, you're awake?" he says, turning toward me. "Thelma of Distinction is in my bed. To what do I owe this pleasure?"

"But are you in love?" I repeat.

"Well, no," he says, matter-of-factly.

Oh.

No. No?

Then why are you there?

Why are you with her?

Why aren't you with the one you love?

"I'm comfortable. It's nice. Pleasant. Uncomplicated. Easy."

Oh.

So it's better to be comfortable. I will never be comfortable for someone. No one will ever want to be with me. I will never have a partner, because I am not comfortable. I am not comfort. I am not a soft pillow. I am not a daily talker. I rarely have the courage to pick up the phone. I am not reliable or consistent. I am moody, dark, introverted. I am liable to hear words that catapult me into space and make me an unpredictable dinner party guest. I say yes when I mean no and I have no intention. I do not rally, I do not get angry, I freeze, fly or swim instead. I do not always speak and sometimes I speak in tongues. I forget people. I have long conversations with people who think they are intimately engaged, but meanwhile I am digging a hole in some cave somewhere and discovering fire while they are talking. No one can ever be sure. I cannot be sure. I am in love right now in this room but I do not know where I will be when I am in the next room. I have a country. I have a home. I have a therapist and a best friend named Molly, but I feel like all I have is a lumpy futon beneath me and a heart breaking in the hands of a man who loves me. He is comfortable. I am not.

Golem Reversing

I feel like I have been run over by a truck. "Is this what real life feels like?" I ask Molly.

"Mmm, hmm," she says. "Sucks, most of the time."

"Well, why . . . "

"Oh, don't go there again. Because when it doesn't, it doesn't, OK?"

"Why are *you* so grumpy?" I snap at her. "Have *you* had your heart trampled upon this week? Hmm?"

"Sorry, you know how much I hate flying. And I miss Sadie."

"Me too. I'm really glad you came with me though, Molly."

"Yeah, I am too. Really glad," she says, smiling at me. "It'll be OK, you know. You needed to do this. His eyes are clean. And so are you."

We are water now. Clean water running though rusted lead pipes.

Later, she asks me, "What do you think of Scotty?"

"Who?"

"My little brother. You met him at the party," she says.

"Oh, yeah. I dunno. He's fine."

"He's into you," she laughs.

"I don't think so," I shake my head.

"What's wrong with him?"

"Well, he's got the same eyes as you, for starters," I say.

"And like I said: What's wrong with him?" she repeats.

"Seems just a little too incestuous," I say.

"Fair enough."

"And besides, I am in love with Patrick. I couldn't imagine being with anyone else."

"Well, if you expect to stop loving him before you're with anyone else, don't hold your breath. It doesn't work that way. I mean you keep on loving, it doesn't go away."

That idea is strange to me. People keep on loving? People keep on loving even if you are not there in their face every day to remind them? People keep on loving even if they no longer see you at all? People keep on loving even if they are loving someone else? Impossible: to believe you can be loved in absence when you don't even know how it feels to be loved when you are there.

—

In here, I tap my breastbone, hoping someone will knock back. I am trying to carry him with me, trying to do what Molly and Dr. N. have both tried to teach me. I think my way through it, with limited success, but then one day I turn on the tap and Patrick runs easily into the sink. He comes to be with me in this strange and wonderful way in my imaginary house full of women and animals. He fills my bath. He moves within my mirror. He watches me as I primp and preen for what turns out to be a disastrous date with Scotty. He follows me through the halls of my house when I return, mortified, from my date. From the series of bad dates I must have because I am not comfort.

—

When I pass my exams, Mary tells me they can convert the back room into an office. I am ecstatic. I call up Molly and she shrieks with joy. "Thelma, I'm coming over right now—put on your wings, girl."

We fly across this city at night, diamond lights glittering beneath us. We sing and swoon in delicate moonlight, our heads softly lit, our hair shining. Our bellies graze against long meadow grasses and our bodies swim through raindrops, mouths first, coming up for air. Sadie plays our toes like piano keys and colours us in with crayons. Molly gives me a painting for my office—a naked woman in the grass falling Christ-like down a hillside. She is big-breasted, voluptuous, her head angled up toward the sky.

—

Heroin is lying on the couch when I come home, even smaller than she was the day before. She is the same woman, just as feisty, only she is shrinking. She is my golem reversing. She has made us stuffed eggplant for dinner, but all the dishes are on the floor because she is no longer tall enough to reach the sink.

Soon she will be a speck swimming in languid liquid comfort. Warm, loved and nestled against me in sleep.

"How was your day?" she asks me.

"Interesting," I say slowly. "I was remembering the time you kicked in the door and tried to stop him—the time you bit his cheek so hard he started bleeding."

"But that was you, Thelma. You were the one who bit him."

"It was me?" I ask, confused.

"Certainly was. You've always been stronger than me."

"Fuck," I marvel. "Strong teeth. Strong mouth."

"Your mouth," she says.

Clench clench these strong teeth in this strong mouth. My mouth. Of my body. In my house. My mouth? Chapped lips swollen and bloody? Dream dreaming wide and thunder? My mouth! My God! This is me speaking. Not mouthing. Not typing and twitching. Not writing a suicide note the length of a novel that will never be finished. I hear voices now but I know they are not the voices of fathers or lovers, or mothers or angels or demons, but the sounds of my own private wars echoing the battles of women before

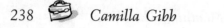

me and near me. No wonder I do not make people comfortable. I am a mirror. I have far too many things to say.

FICT Gib
Gibb, Camilla.
Mouthing the words /

$22.00 05/16/01 AGM-9556

DATE DUE